DARK MALICE

CHARLI CROSS SERIES: BOOK FOUR

MARY STONE
DONNA BERDEL

Copyright © 2022 by Mary Stone

All rights reserved.

No part of this book may be reproduced in any form or by any electronic or mechanical means, including information storage and retrieval systems, without written permission from the author, except for the use of brief quotations in a book review.

❦ Created with Vellum

DESCRIPTION

In the face of malice, evil is spawned.

Savannah Police Detective Charli Cross thought she'd seen it all. But when Charli and her partner, Matthew Church, are called in on a missing persons report from a local funeral home, she realizes this may be the most bizarre and perplexing case yet. Not only are three funeral home employees missing, but one left her car in the funeral home parking lot overnight. Stranger still, the cremator was filled with the ashes of two people, even though all the funeral home's "guests" are accounted for.

Where are the missing employees? Who was burned to ash? And why?

As Charli and Matthew investigate, the questions continue to stack up. With no DNA evidence to identify the cremains, their only clue is a diary filled with cryptic descriptions and video footage that's as mysterious as the case itself.

When the puzzle pieces begin to fit together, one thing becomes clear. The closer Charli gets to the killer, the more certain she is that she or her partner might be the next one to burn.

By turns riveting and disconcerting, Dark Malice is the fourth book in the Charli Cross Series from bestselling author Mary Stone—guaranteed to make you think twice before you make a deal with the devil.

1

Candace Redding tapped her pen against the front of her notebook like windshield wipers during a downpour. The black ink began to blur in the pen's clear casing, much like Candace's mind as she worried about what she was about to do.

How had it come to this?

The first time they had asked for her help, the extra money had seemed like a dream come true. On a secretary's salary, half her meals consisted of ramen noodles while trying to make rent. She'd never been handed such a large stack of bills at one time.

She dropped her face into her hands. What had she done in exchange for all that cash?

Sell her soul.

No, Candace wasn't proud of what she'd been doing, but the money had gone a long way toward making her feel better. Or it used to, anyway. These days, the price on her soul had increased. A girl had to keep up with inflation.

She scoffed and fingered the five-thousand-dollar tennis bracelet she'd bought for herself while singing "7 Rings" in the jewelry store. In reality, the only thing that had inflated in Candace's life was her taste for luxury.

After selling her soul, she might have gone a bit overboard, but having come from a poor family who shopped in thrift stores and lived off food stamps, Candace had been due a little bit of the good life. At least that's what she'd told herself.

When that first payment had hit her hands, she promised herself she'd never buy another pack of ramen or eat at a fast-food joint. If she wanted takeout, she'd grab steak from West Lounge.

She'd been so happy to know those days were behind her.

She lived in a beautiful apartment. And forget the beat-up Toyota Corolla that had lived through Clinton's presidency. She now drove a Mercedes with a push-start ignition.

And now?

Now, the money that had once appeared as large as the Empire State Building had become a puddle to her.

She needed more.

No…she deserved more.

Despite living in the lap of luxury, Candace had slowly become trapped in the cycle she was stuck in while broke. She lived from paycheck to paycheck again, trying to pay for her luxury apartment.

Why should she needlessly struggle to pay the bills again? Surely her time was worth more than that now. For these men, she was essential. At most jobs, one was replaceable, but not at this position. At least, it wouldn't be easy to find a substitute.

Candace glanced at the cherrywood grandfather clock ticking away the seconds in the mortuary lobby. The normally innocuous clicking of the second hand grated on her ears. It may as well have been nails on a chalkboard.

They'd arrive any minute now, and Candace had to be ready to make her demands.

She swallowed hard. It was five minutes until one in the morning. Maybe today wasn't the right day, after all.

Though she was normally a hard sleeper, she'd woken up at exactly 5:55 yesterday morning. Damn fives. That was her unlucky number.

On her fifth birthday, she'd fallen off the pony ride at the petting zoo and broken her wrist. In the fifth grade, she'd contracted mono and spent fifteen weeks home in bed, barely able to stay awake. And somehow, every May, Candace managed to experience a minor catastrophe. Last May, she had gotten appendicitis and needed emergency surgery. The May before that was the month her grandma had passed away from an ugly battle with Alzheimer's.

Candace gingerly massaged her temples, willing the pulsing headache to fade away. Hadn't she talked this through with her therapist? Her tendency toward superstition was just another manifestation of her OCD. She couldn't continue to give in to the intrusive thoughts.

Waking up to all fives on her alarm clock was not an omen of bad things to come, but an inconsequential coincidence. Would she even have noticed if it had been any other day?

"Stop it."

Her voice was loud in the quiet office. She knew what she was doing...pleading for reasons to back out of what she was about to do.

But she wouldn't because she had to do this. If she didn't, she'd spend the rest of her days wishing she had enough money to support her now-luxurious lifestyle.

What an idiot she'd been to accept the original cash payment. Why hadn't she considered the mental toll this was going to take? Before this, she'd never even needed a therapist.

Candace hadn't always suffered from fear of being haunted, hearing whispers of ghosts in her ear as she fidgeted at her desk. The mortuary didn't bother her when she first started working there. In fact, it had been a place of comfort. But back then, she didn't believe any of the deceased had a reason to be angry with her.

Candace's regrets stirred in her stomach, a rapid whirlpool of anguish and sunken dreams. If she could go back, if she could refuse the money, she would do it in a heartbeat. But unless she found a time machine, there was no way she could end this. They had explained to her that once she agreed, she'd never be able to stop, not without losing her life.

So, if she couldn't stop, if she had to continue to help them, at least she could get a more comfortable life out of it. Living in a constant state of heightened stress while simultaneously worrying about money wasn't what Candace had in mind when she'd taken the job.

The burner phone she carried echoed out its familiar ring, and Candace shot up in response. Her fingers shook as she lifted it to her ear.

"Kirkland Funeral Home. This is Candace speaking." Though it was nearly one in the morning, and there was only one person who could be calling, Candace answered the phone this way out of habit.

"Five minutes." The hollow voice said nothing else before hanging up.

Another damn five.

Candace painstakingly pocketed the phone while her pounding heartbeat radiated into her temples. She would have to do this in five minutes. What could go wrong?

She couldn't believe she'd even asked the question.

"What could go wrong?" She snorted to herself.

Well, she was dealing with cold-blooded killers, so they could always murder her. But they wouldn't do that. That would be an illogical move on their part.

Right?

There was no reason to kill her when they could continue to use her. Candace was indispensable to them, a necessary component of their operation. Because of this, they would give her the money she was going to ask for.

After that, things would get better. She would at least be able to forgo financial stress.

You can do this.

Letting out a shaky breath, Candace stood and straightened her pleated plaid skirt. She traced the black and gray lines with her fingertips before moving to the mirror to check her hair and makeup. The ruby lipstick made her green eyes pop like pine needles against red Christmas ribbon. Her auburn bob sat in a perfect line on her shoulders. Candace knew these gentlemen didn't work with her just because she was attractive, but that didn't mean looking her best wouldn't still help during these negotiations.

Her skirt swayed from side to side as she walked into the office where the bay of security cameras sat and turned off the camera for the side door.

Oops.

She made a mental note to turn the camera back on after her visitors had left. After that, she strode across the lobby to make sure those doors were locked. When she flipped the switch, the overhead lights vanished to match the dark September night outside. There was only the lamp of the back room shining through the cracks in the door to guide her.

She was technically supposed to leave the lobby light off the entire time she was waiting so that nobody noticed someone was in the funeral home offices, but it bothered her so severely that she couldn't sit still in the pitch black. As if what she had to do wasn't eerie enough.

The back room had no windows. It was fine to leave that light on, so she waited by the side door, running her hands down her skirt to keep the dampness at bay.

Knock. Knock. Knock.

Candace jumped, though she'd known the sound was coming. Time to put her game face on.

She held the door open to allow the large man on the other side entrance. "Hurry, before someone sees you."

A black body bag flung over broad shoulders blended in with the dark clothes the man was wearing. "You think I'd let anyone see me? Use your brain. Are we good to go?"

Candace hurried toward the back of the building, to the cremator room. She paused at the door. "We are, but I was hoping I could talk to you first."

"Don't you think this is a little more urgent?" He readjusted the weight he was carrying. He didn't have even the hint of an expression on his face.

In her head, she'd nicknamed him "No-Face," like the monster in her niece's favorite childhood movie *Spirited Away*. Although she hadn't seen the film in years, she remembered the character vividly. This man also had an obsession with money, much like the *Spirited Away* monster.

Candace was never allowed to call them by name, and besides, she only knew the name of one of her bosses. They'd assured her the less she knew about the organization, the safer she would be.

And that suited Candace fine. Knowing the names of everyone she worked for wouldn't ease her superstitious mind. Neither would it help assuage her guilt to know that these people, like the one tossed over No-Face's shoulder, may have spouses, children, and families who were waiting for them.

Still, over the last four years, she'd managed to take detailed notes on each body for her own security.

"This is urgent too. Look, I don't think I can do this anymore, un-unless..." Candace had practiced this line multiple times in her bathroom mirror, but the words weren't coming out as smoothly as they had when it was only her and her reflection. Despite her best efforts to swallow the stutter forming in her words, they reverberated out of her throat.

No-Face towered over her. "Unless what?"

"Unless you can compensate me a little better." The words tumbled out of Candace's mouth as a bead of sweat trickled down the small of her back. "This is a lot on me, you know. It takes hours in the middle of the night for this process to take place. If anyone ever found out about this, I'd lose more than my job. I'd end up in federal prison with a whole slew of charges."

His face didn't give even a hint of what he was thinking, but it never did. He was the most stoic of the group. But with that came a calm demeanor that the others didn't share. If Candace had to make this request, she would rather make it to him. No-Face may be a formidable man, but at least with him, there was no instantaneous rage to deal with.

"And how much more are you expecting?" He barreled past her and into the crematorium, giving Candace no indication of his thoughts. No-Face unceremoniously plopped the body bag down on the stainless-steel loading table.

She followed him inside. "I was thinking...d-double, maybe?" Candace hadn't intended for the answer to come out with such a squeaky tone.

"Double, huh?"

The voice came from behind her, and fear crawled down

Candace's spine. She froze, her body becoming a statue. She swallowed hard, but it didn't rid her of the softball-sized lump in her throat.

She wasn't expecting *him* to be here. He often wasn't. And if she had known he was going to be, she wouldn't have asked this today. She couldn't ask him. It had to be anyone but this man.

An ache formed in her stomach, unlike anything she'd ever experienced before as she turned to him, lifting her chin. "I m-mean, I'm open to negotiations."

"You warmed this thing up?" The foul man Candace thought of as "Slick" pointed toward the cremator. His dark hair was always slicked back, with never a hair out of place.

"Of c-course. I've been here for thirty minutes, as always. As you know, I've n-never been late. I show up on only twenty-four hours' notice. I'm a g-great asset to you."

Why was she talking to him like this was a job interview? She sounded like a seventeen-year-old trying to nab a barista position at the local coffee shop.

No-Face stepped backward, no longer taking part in the conversation. This only made the lump in Candace's throat grow larger. The shrimp alfredo she'd had for dinner threatened to come back up.

Screw her damn therapist. She should have listened to the fives!

With the other man leaning back against the wall, she was left to deal with the body while this psychopath breathed down her neck. His hot, sticky breath enveloped her. It only quickened her already racing heart.

"We need that bag back."

Maybe Candace shouldn't discuss the money any further. After all, if these fiends needed to reuse body bags, maybe their funds were more limited than she'd imagined. Why hadn't she thought of that before?

She couldn't go back in time, though. She prayed that if she followed his directions closely, he'd forget about it and let this go.

The metal zipper chilled her fingertips. When it separated, it revealed a young man with a dark goatee and a single bullet hole in his forehead.

Still inches behind her, she swore that Slick sniffed her hair. "So, if we don't double your pay, this is the last body you're going to take for us, huh?"

So much for not discussing the money.

Candace could back down now, take back her request for more cash. But if she did that, she would never receive more. It would end the conversation for good.

Despite the tremor in her legs at the mere sight of this man, she couldn't do that. Living in financial straits while harboring the shame of her actions would not lead to a fulfilling life. She had to stand by her request.

She rested her hands at her sides, resisting the urge to fidget with her watch. "I just d-don't think I can. Last time, I was nearly caught. I need to make sure I'm taken care of."

The way this funeral home was set up was perfect for Slick's needs because the cremator was located on a different floor than the embalming room, which was in the basement. The door between the basement and this floor was always locked at night so the interns and night workers didn't have access to the offices. But last week, the door had been left unlocked and Candace hadn't thought to check it. It was only by the grace of God that she'd heard the door click open before one of the night workers had found her scraping ashes into a box.

Slick's thin mouth twitched at the right corner before forming a sinister smile. "You want to be taken care of, huh?"

Candace let out a shaky breath. "I d-do."

Slick stepped toward her. "You gonna just stand there, or are you gonna fry this guy?"

She jumped into motion, rushing to do as instructed, as Slick stepped over to where No-Face stood. Her hands shook badly as she removed the body bag from the man who, in addition to the bullet to the head, had been shot in the chest at least twice that she could see. A couple missing fingers showed that his last moments in life had been torturous.

One.

Two.

Three.

The minutes ticked by as she worked, and beads of sweat formed on her brow. *How long could she stand the silence?*

Candace couldn't take it anymore. When she was finished prepping the dead man, she opened her mouth, ready to tell Slick she didn't need any more cash, when he spoke up.

"Well, if you want to be taken care of, we'll take care of you."

Relief washed over Candace, and she let out a nervous laugh, turning to face Slick again. "R-really?"

"Absolutely." He glanced at No-Face. "You wanna help me take care of her?"

Both men stepped forward, and in a split second, her relief turned to dread. The world around her moved in slow motion, as if she were a movie character about to experience her last moments.

Was she?

She flung both hands up, and they shook wildly in front of her face. "No, wait! Please, it's fine. I'll keep w-working for you at our agreed price. It's no big d-deal. Really!"

Candace squeezed her eyes shut, praying this was only an intimidation tactic to keep her in line. Strong arms grabbed her, powerful fingers closing around her elbows like a vise.

In that moment, the hope that had burned in her chest was snuffed out like a light.

"No!" She kicked and screamed, but her own voice was foreign before becoming muffled by the hand slapped over her mouth.

Slick grabbed Candace's chin and leaned down until they were eye to eye. "I don't take well to threats. Can't trust people that threaten me, either. Let's just say you won't be working for us anymore."

Panic exploded in Candace's chest, and she had an instant urge to vomit. She wrenched her chin free of the vile man's grasp, turning wildly to No-Face. "Don't do this." She managed to pull his fingers from her mouth just enough that she could speak. "P-please. You can t-trust me, I swear. I'll do whatever you w-want."

But her pleas fell on deaf ears. She knew he listened to the demands of the boss. He always had.

As though she weighed no more than a child, No-Face lifted her until she was sprawled across the dead man on the loading table. With a push of a button, the cremator door slid open. A gust of hot lava rushed toward Candace's feet.

No!

She screamed again, and blood filled her mouth as the hand slammed back down, cutting her lips on her teeth.

This couldn't be how her life ended. She had so much left to do. Since she was a little girl, she'd wanted to get married. Candace had never fallen in love, never had kids. All she'd done was chase money endlessly, and now it would cost her the most precious thing she had. Her life.

"Please! I don't want to die!" Her sobs were heavy, her body heaving as she wailed. She was a defenseless rabbit caught in a rushing river, drowning in the waves.

Mustering every ounce of strength she had, Candace writhed as hard as she could. But she was one hundred and ten pounds soaking wet, and these men were nothing but muscle. Moving her arms against them only created a burning friction on her skin.

Tears blurring her vision, Candace slammed the heel of her hand into Slick's nose.

Rage contorted his face, and his grip loosened around her arms, allowing a flame of hope to ignite in her chest once more. Twisting her body, she managed to lift her leg and knee him straight in the groin with all her might.

He stumbled backward in pain, releasing Candace from his grip. "You little bitch!"

Wrenching away from No-Face, Candace rolled off the dead man and sprinted toward the door. If she could just make it outside, she could hide somewhere and call the police. She was going to make it. She was going to live.

An iron fist came out of nowhere, yanking her to a stop before dragging her toward the cremator once more. "It's over."

Candace jerked and kicked, but the monster's arms of steel continued to drag her across the floor.

"Noooo!"

Slick joined his partner, grabbing Candace's legs. "I hate that it has to end this way. You've been so...helpful." A slow smile spread across his wicked face.

As they moved her closer to the cremator, Candace clawed at everything she saw along the way, but she was grasping for straws.

She'd heard that, in one's last moments, their life flashed before their eyes, but she'd just assumed that was a figure of speech. Now forced to look death in the face, Candace's memories came rushing to the surface. Her sixth birthday party, when her father had taken her to ride a horse for the first time. The last time she'd held her mother, whom she hadn't visited in ages.

Why did she never go see her? What had been more important than family?

Salty tears streaked down her cheeks. "Please! P-please don't do this. I'll do anything you ask. *Anything.* I—"

She shrieked as heat seared the bottoms of her feet as she was tossed onto the dead man again, and the loading table began to move into the primary chamber. Hands held her in place, and she was powerless to stop the men from pushing her inside.

Mama. Oh, Mama, I'm so scared.

Flames came to life as the fire found new food to consume.

I'm so sorry.

As the flames melted her flesh, all her thoughts disappeared. There was only searing agony, unlike anything she'd ever known.

Her screams echoed against the cremator walls…until they didn't anymore.

2

Un-freaking-believable.

Detective Charlotte Cross took one last longing glance at her computer screen before exiting the browser. As much as she wanted to daydream about a tropical vacation, she had a case to investigate.

She pushed her desk chair back and turned to her partner. "So much for a break between cases."

Detective Matthew Church flashed Charli a grin as he headed out the door to catch up with their boss. "That'll happen when pigs fly."

Charli hurried to catch up with Matthew. For the thousandth time, Charli wished she had longer legs. She stepped through the doorframe of their boss's office. "Kirkland Funeral Home, huh?" Charli had heard of the place, although she'd never had a reason to go inside.

Sergeant Ruth Morris was already seated at her desk. "That's the one. Evidently, three employees didn't show up for work this morning."

"That hardly seems like an issue requiring police

assistance." Matthew echoed Charli's thoughts as he lowered himself into a chair across from Ruth.

The sergeant straightened a stack of papers on her desk. "It wouldn't be. Except that one of their cars is still in the parking lot, and something about a body being stolen. The 911 caller wasn't very clear."

"Who the hell steals bodies from a mortuary?" Charli glanced between her boss and her partner.

The sergeant rolled her chocolate brown eyes. "That's what I want you two to find out. A few officers are down there now, and out of 'an abundance of caution,'" Ruth air quoted the words, "the first officer to arrive established the funeral home as a crime scene. I want you guys out there five minutes ago."

Matthew rose from his chair. "Then we're already driving. Aren't we, Charli?"

Charli pulled her keys out of her pocket and dangled them in the air. "Sure are."

There was a bit of pep in Matthew's step on the way to the car.

"Relieved you're not stuck answering phones?" Charli sped up to keep his stride.

"Not only do I not have to answer phones, but there are no gruesome bodies waiting to be identified. Sounds like a pretty good day to me."

Matthew couldn't stand gore, but Charli rarely had an issue with it. Not that she enjoyed seeing mangled bodies, but it didn't cause her any undue stress. To her, a dead body deserved her complete attention so she could gather the clues it provided and do her best to make sure whoever hurt it was caught and brought to justice.

With a grin, Charli opened the car door for Matthew, since his right arm was full of stitches from their last case, when the perpetrator had unexpectedly pulled a knife and attempted to plunge the blade into Matthew's chest. His arm had blocked the blow, but he hadn't escaped without injury. Today was his first day back on the job, and he seemed delighted to have managed to escape desk duty for a new case.

Matthew bowed into an exaggerated curtsy. "What a gentleman you are."

Charli stifled a laugh, the grin growing wider. "Don't get used to it."

Kirkland Funeral Home was only ten minutes from the precinct. Charli was familiar with it because one of her favorite Chinese food places stood right across the street. Too bad it was nine in the morning. A little early for a container of Kung Pao shrimp.

Yellow police tape surrounded a black Mercedes in the funeral home parking lot, and Charli assumed it belonged to one of the employees who had failed to show up for work. Officer Donnie Langston stood outside the entrance, logbook in hand.

Charli took the book to sign in before holding it out for her partner to sign. "Hello, Officer. What have you got for us? Something about a missing body?"

The lanky officer rubbed a finger across his neatly trimmed mustache, the same shade as his blond comb-over. "Well, since that call was made, we've managed to straighten a few things out."

Charli frowned. "What do you mean?"

"When the manager came in this morning, he found the cremator still on, though it wasn't supposed to be used the previous day or night. At first, he believed it was a mistake of one of his employees, until he found enough ashes inside for two bodies."

Matthew was still scrawling his awkward left-handed signature when his head snapped up. "So, no one stole a body from the mortuary?"

Officer Langston reached for the logbook as Matthew finished signing in, a sheepish smile creeping onto his face. "Well, that's what I thought initially. There was a bit of… confusion. Anyway, it's a long story, and the funeral director is in his office waiting to speak to you."

Charli flashed the officer a smile. "We'll go speak with him now. Thanks."

The director's office was pretty much what Charli expected of a funeral home administrator. It was a dreary room with deep green walls that almost looked black at first glance. His dark wood desk was empty, devoid of any family photos or decorations. Putting up photographs of loved ones in a place where people would be grieving their own family members probably wasn't advisable. Still, the room could've been designed to be a little more inviting.

A tall man with strawberry blond hair that had more white than red sat at the desk. Charli imagined the man's hair had been a brilliant shade of auburn in his youth. "You must be Detective Cross and Detective Church. I've seen you guys on the news. You helped with the Mowery case, right?"

Charli didn't much enjoy being recognized this way. This was one of the many reasons she hated doing press conferences. "We are, yes."

He stood up from behind his desk to extend a hand. "I'm Bernie Cobb."

Matthew was the first to shake it. "What is your position at this establishment, Mr. Cobb?"

The man smiled and smoothed his crimson tie. "I'm the director. I handle the day-to-day operations, since the owners are rarely here."

Charli took a seat in one of the black leather chairs in front of the executive desk. "My partner and I would like to ask you a few questions, Mr. Cobb." The director nodded his acquiescence. "Can you tell us what time you arrived at the funeral home this morning?"

His brow furrowed. "I've already explained all of this to the other officers."

Matthew settled into the seat next to Charli. "We understand, but we have to keep our own records."

The director sighed. "Well, I came in at eight as I do every morning. I was expecting three employees to be here already, but only Candace Redding's car was in the lot. I wasn't surprised by that, considering she's my most punctual employee." He leaned back in his chair, concern marring his features. "Until I came in, and she was nowhere to be found."

Charli jotted the details down in her notebook. "I noticed a security camera on top of the back door marked 'employees only' when we came in. Is that camera functional? Have you checked it to see when Ms. Redding arrived?"

Cobb brushed away an imaginary speck of dust from the corner of his desk. "It is, and I did. She came in a little before twelve-thirty this morning."

Charli's pen froze in its spot. She glanced up from her notes. "Is it normal for your employees to be here in the middle of the night?"

Bernie shrugged. "We run three shifts, so there are employees here around the clock. And although Candace typically works from eight to five, it's not unusual for her to show up at odd hours to do paperwork. As I said, she is a very reliable employee."

That made no sense whatsoever. Even if Candace was an excellent employee, what kind of person rolled out of bed in the middle of the night and went to their job to do paperwork? Even if she was diligent, why wouldn't she just stay late after her shift or come in early the next day?

Matthew cleared his throat. "We're going to need that security camera footage."

The funeral director leaned down and rummaged in a desk drawer, pulling out a black leather-bound book and setting it on the middle of his desk. "I already gave it to the other officer, but you're going to see exactly what I did. Candace shows up at 12:24 this morning, walks in from her car, and then never leaves."

The detectives made brief eye contact, and Charli knew they were on the same wavelength. If Candace didn't leave, one of the bodies in that cremator could be hers.

"Is it possible for someone to put their own body into the cremator?" Charli didn't want to ask about whether Candace could lock herself in specifically. She saw no reason to make that assumption aloud, but the director filled in the gaps for her.

"Are you asking if Candace could have cremated herself? I mean, anyone can throw their own body in, but you can't close the door from the inside, and it was locked shut."

Mr. Cobb was awfully blasé about the possibility that his secretary had been burned to a crisp. But perhaps that was what working with death day in and day out did to a person. After all, hadn't Charli and Matthew acquired a very dark sense of humor after years on the job?

Charli wasn't leaning toward suicide, but she had to rule out every possibility. Burning to death wasn't how most sane people would choose to die. But sometimes, when a person was suffering from psychosis, they made some very odd choices. This early in the investigation, the detectives had to keep an open mind.

Matthew leaned forward, putting his good arm on his knee. "And did you see anyone else come and go on the security footage?"

"Nope. It was only Candace." The director picked a piece of lint from his dark suit jacket. "Though, a strange thing did happen."

Charli loved when strange things happened because those incidences were usually a clue. "What's that?"

"Well, the camera for the employee entrance stopped working at 12:55 this morning."

Well…well…well…it was, in fact, another clue, though this one might create more questions than answers.

"Only that camera?" Matthew asked.

Bernie nodded. "I turned it back on when I noticed it wasn't functioning."

Dammit. In doing so, Bernie probably destroyed any fingerprints they could have taken, but Charli made a note to test the system for prints anyway.

The detectives exchanged another brief glance, and Matthew straightened in his seat. "You said there were enough ashes for two bodies, correct? Is it possible the other burned body came from within the funeral home?"

Bernie's face contorted in dismay. "Oh, heavens no. That would be impossible. We keep a very detailed record of all our deceased and what services they're scheduled for. Besides, it's illegal to cremate multiple bodies at the same time in the United States." The director took out a logbook from a drawer behind his desk and slid it over to Charli. "All our deceased have been accounted for, and there was no one on the schedule to be cremated last night or this morning. Neither of those cremated bodies was one of our…guests."

What a word.

Charli flipped to a new page in her notebook. "So, if one of your employees couldn't have cremated themselves and all your, um, guests, are accounted for, how could at least two bodies' worth of ashes be discovered in the cremator?"

Blind spots. Charli already knew the answer but wanted the director's input.

Bernie ran a hand through his hair. "Detectives, though security is a primary concern, there are blind spots within our monitoring system that would make it possible for someone to leave or arrive without being spotted. If someone were to walk up to the back door, for example, from the left sidewalk, they would not be detected on our footage. Those bodies could belong to anyone."

But how would they have gotten inside? And why?

"How many entrances are in the building?"

Bernie sighed as he pulled out a map of the funeral home to answer Charli's question. "We have five doors. Our main lobby entrance as well as the entrance where our hearses receive the deceased following a memorial service. Then there is a side door near the crematorium, which is used for the office staff who work on this floor. Those three are all on this level."

Charli examined the map. "And downstairs?"

Bernie pointed at a door. "This is the entrance and exit for mortuary staff." He pointed again. "And this one is used for receiving the deceased."

Matthew tapped that part of the map. "Who uses those doors?"

The funeral director gave another long sigh, seeming to be annoyed with the question. "Hearses, ambulances, coroner vans."

Five doors with blind spots would widen the scope of the case a great deal. If anyone could walk in or out undetected, then Candace may have walked out of the building herself. If that were the case, it was possible she wasn't one of the deceased bodies, after all. Though it would be strange for her not to go back to her car after leaving. Still, Charli had to keep in mind all possibilities.

"You said two other employees failed to show up for work today, correct?" Matthew took the floor while Charli wrote down details about the security camera. "Can we get their names?"

"That would be Jacob Pernell and Elwood Sanders. Elwood does custodial and maintenance work for us. Honestly, he's a bit of an airhead, and it wouldn't be the first time he failed to show up. But I keep him around because he does a good job when he's here. Jacob, like Candace, is usually punctual, though. He's one of my assistants. I've got an employee directory with their numbers and addresses."

Charli stopped her note-taking to meet Bernie's eye. "We're going to need that entire directory to contact other employees as well."

Just because these three were the ones who failed to show up for work today didn't mean other employees weren't potentially involved. Anyone who had access to the building was a potential suspect.

The director flashed a patronizing smile that didn't quite reach his eyes. "Absolutely. I'll make sure you have the contact information for all twenty-eight of them."

Matthew lifted his eyebrows. "You have twenty-eight employees at this funeral home?"

Charli was just as surprised. How many people did it take to run this small building?

"Detective Church, we're one of the busiest funeral homes in Savannah. Every body that is unclaimed by a family member is sent to us by the county. As I mentioned, we're open every day, twenty-four hours a day. We have receptionists, secretaries, morticians, custodial staff, director's assistants, interns, and other staff members."

Evidently, Charli had no idea how much manpower it took to keep a funeral home running.

It seemed she was about to find out.

3

Although Mr. Cobb had to excuse himself to meet with a family to discuss funeral arrangements, Charli wasn't quite done with him. She and Matthew were surprised to find that a forensics team had already been called and were huddled around the cremator.

Not long ago, Charli had watched a YouTube video about what happened to bodies during a cremation process. The video had just appeared on her feed, and because she was always interested in anything gory, she'd watched the entire thing. That knowledge would come in handy today.

She might not know all the ins and outs of how a funeral home was run, but she had learned human DNA was fried before it reached the cremator's 1,800 degrees. If a body was burned on a bonfire, bone and dental fragments could remain because a normal fire wouldn't get hot enough to turn the entire corpse to ash.

But these cremators were designed to do just that. And any bits of metal—such as screws or pins that the individual had surgically implanted during their life—would be ground down by a specially designed processor before the remains were given to the family. Nobody wanted to spread their loved one's ashes in the ocean and see a chunk floating away.

That meant there would be no DNA. Still, Charli held onto hope that perhaps DNA had been left elsewhere at the scene.

Charli snapped a pair of gloves on her hands. "Find anything useful to help with an ID?"

A member of the forensics team shook his head. "We just arrived, so there isn't much we've found yet. Normally, a body is cremated with a steel disc for identification, but there were none here. Which would mean either someone made a grave mistake during the cremation process, or these bodies were never supposed to be burned in the first place."

Matthew leaned down to glance at the pile of ash. "According to the funeral director, it's the latter."

The forensics tech rubbed his cheek on his shoulder, not wanting to touch his face with his gloved hand, Charli imagined. "We were able to find pieces of two cell phones, though. We've got a couple sim cards, though both are unreadable."

That was valuable information, regardless. Even if they couldn't extract any information out of the phones, whoever threw them in there must have not realized that the devices wouldn't completely burn up in a cremator. Did that mean it was unlikely anyone who used this machine regularly was responsible for burning the two bodies?

Another clue.

Charli likely wouldn't glean any more information from these ashes. The thought was disappointing because, with no leads, she and Matthew were going to have to interview all twenty-eight of the employees at the funeral home.

That was going to be a good time. Even if she and her partner split up and took half the employees individually, it would take a while to get through everyone.

Charli peeked into the cremator herself. Why did Cobb

think there were two bodies involved? There was certainly an excess of ash in the machine, but what would she know? Her YouTube video hadn't gone into that type of detail.

Could it be that one of these bodies belonged to Candace and the other to another missing employee? Perhaps Candace came into work in the middle of the night and stumbled upon something she shouldn't have known about that was going on inside the funeral home, and she was killed for it? Then the next employee to walk in early this morning met the same fate? But if that theory was true, where was the second employee's car?

The questions were stacking up.

According to Cobb, there was no way to tell when the cremator was turned on or what time the bodies had been thrown in. The only thing he could say definitively was that it wasn't on when he left last night, but was running when he arrived in the morning. Which meant that somehow the machine had been turned on during the night.

But that timeline left things wide open, as did the fact that the security cameras couldn't identify anyone who walked in through the door without arriving in the parking lot. There was a lot of digging to be done before Charli could even begin to scratch the surface of what had happened in this hollow, metal room.

"What's going on here?" A male voice came from behind Charli.

Matthew turned to the source, his eyebrows raised. "Who are you, exactly?"

"I'm Finn Carter." The slender man swiveled his head between Charli and Matthew. "I'm doing an internship here at the funeral home. What happened?"

Finn's green eyes went wide at the sight of the neon crime scene tape. He pushed his shaggy brown hair off his forehead. Charli guessed he couldn't have been older than twenty-two.

"Mr. Carter, can you step outside with us?" Matthew motioned Finn toward the door to the hallway. "Got an ID on you?"

Finn fished his wallet out of his back pocket to hand it to Matthew. "I don't understand. Has something happened?" The younger man continued to look over his shoulder at the forensics team as they moved out into the hallway and headed toward the parking lot.

"We're not at liberty to discuss that right now." According to his license, Finn was twenty-one. Charli had no intention of telling this college-age kid what was going on. Their previous case had been publicized through TikTok. The last thing she needed was Finn going on social media and gossiping about the case. "You said you're interning here?"

"Yes. I'm training to be a mortician, and intern hours are required by my program."

"Do you happen to have keys to the building?" Matthew towered over Finn's five-foot, eight-inch stature.

Finn flicked his hair off his forehead again. "No. I only come here when I'm scheduled, and someone is always here to teach me."

"Mr. Carter, can you tell me about what you were doing last night, beginning at seven p.m.?" Though it was pretty certain that the secretary hadn't arrived until after midnight, Charli preferred to expand the hours to learn what potential suspects had been up to prior to a crime.

Finn shoved his hands in his pockets. "Uh, well, I was just waking up at seven."

Matthew cocked his head to the right. "She asked you about seven p.m., not seven a.m."

"I know. But my program requires you to simulate the hours that a mortician has to work, so they have me doing the night shift at the lab all week. I woke up at seven p.m., had dinner on campus, and started my shift. I was there until six-thirty this morning."

Well, if that was true, it ruled him out as a suspect. But why was he here now?

"Can anyone confirm that?" Charli imagined, at the very least, that the university had security cameras in their lab.

The intern nodded. "Sure, my professor and my lab partner could tell you. But why? What happened here last night?"

Matthew dodged the question. "So, you got off one shift at six-thirty and arrive here for another one? That's pretty brutal."

As if on cue, the intern yawned. "Yeah, but a man's gotta do what a man's gotta do."

Charli didn't correct him with a reminder that most women worked far more hours in a day than a man. "How many days a week do you work here?"

"Usually just three. I've been doing it for the past two months." Finn stepped to the side, continuing to peer in the direction of the funeral home door.

Matthew kicked the door shut. "While you've been working here, have you observed any interpersonal drama in the workplace? Any employees who disliked one another?"

Finn fidgeted with his hair again before shoving his hands back in his pants pockets. "No, not at all, but nobody really talks to me. Everyone else who works here is a lot older, and they only address me when it's necessary for the job. I'm not really friends with anyone out here."

Well, this could be a dead end, but Charli expected most of their employee interviews would be. With twenty-eight people to talk to, most of them would be oblivious to the crime that occurred last night. Hell, there was still the chance that no employee had been involved with this incident at all.

Charli put her notebook in her jacket pocket. "I doubt you'll be doing any intern work this morning but go through the lobby to ask the funeral director. Please do not enter anywhere you see crime scene tape again."

Finn gave a reluctant nod before walking around the edge of the building to the front.

Charli scanned the parking lot. "Where the hell is Officer Langston? Shouldn't he be out here making sure that people aren't walking into the building?"

Matthew pointed to the black Mercedes across the lot. "Looks like he's over there."

Langston was standing just outside the crime scene tape around the vehicle. Charli groaned before making her way over. "Officer Langston, did you realize an employee just walked right into the crime scene?" Charli's voice gave the officer a start.

"What? I swear I was keeping an eye on the door, but I was curious to see if Ms. Redding had left anything in her vehicle. I'm sorry. I'll return to my post immediately."

Charli wanted to be mad at the younger officer, but she'd done similar things back when she was a beat cop. Whenever she'd been given a menial task, she was bored to tears and found herself thinking about the crime scene as a detective would. Still, it may be boring, but holding onto the logbook and ensuring nobody entered the crime scene was an important job.

Matthew nudged the officer away from the car. "Yeah... go do your job."

Ignoring her partner's gruffness, Charli peered into one of the car's windows, being careful not to touch anything. It was almost completely empty. There wasn't so much as a Starbucks drink in the cupholder.

It seemed almost too clean. Charli liked to stay organized, but even she had random items stashed around her vehicle.

"Either this woman is a total neat freak, or someone cleaned out this car."

Matthew scanned the Mercedes from where he stood. "If they did, we'll see it on the security cameras, right?"

Charli shrugged. "Unless the camera that was turned off is the one pointed this way. We need to review that footage as soon as we're back at the precinct." Though that was going to be a while if they started interviewing employees right away.

She was just about to head back into the building to get started when Charli glimpsed a man opening the gate to the cemetery adjacent to the funeral home.

"Hey, do you think he has a key to the building?" Charli pointed across the long stretch of grass.

Matthew started heading that way. "It's worth asking."

Already, the sun on the gravel of the parking lot was reflecting heat back up, and Charli was relieved to reach the grass. The chilly morning dew and shade from nearby trees took a few degrees off the current temperature.

Charli waved the graveyard attendant down. "Excuse me."

The graying man with rosy cheeks returned the wave with enthusiasm. He had the opposite demeanor of the funeral director. His grin went from one ear to the other, radiating light. Evidently, working above dead bodies didn't bring down his spirit.

"How can I help you two this morning? Are you looking for a relative, because I've got a map in my back pocket here, and as long as you know the plot number..." The man's words flew out of his mouth at the speed of light. Charli had to cut him off to get a word in edgewise.

"No, actually, we'd like to talk to you. I'm Detective Cross, and this is my partner, Detective Church. Do you work at the cemetery?"

"Oh, sure do! I'm Gary Stinett. Been working here for a

good ten years. What can I do for you?" If the man's grin got any wider, Charli was sure his face would split.

Once again, Charli reached in her pocket for her notebook. "Do you mind if my partner and I ask you a few questions?"

The jovial man leaned against the fence. "Not at all."

A bit of dew flung from the grass near Matthew's foot as he stepped forward. "Do you happen to have the keys to this building?"

"The funeral home? Oh, yes. They've got a custodial closet of sorts attached to the outside of the building where I keep my supplies. Lawn mower, nutrients for the flower garden, brushes for me to clean off dirty gravestones, and the like."

Admittedly, it was hard to believe this overly cheery graveyard attendant could be a possible criminal. But Charli had spent enough time reading about serial killers to know they often seemed charismatic and charming. Nobody was going to be off her list of suspects without a solid alibi.

Matthew shifted his weight to one leg, gingerly massaging the stitches in his right arm. "And what were you doing from seven last night to seven this morning, Mr. Stinett?"

The cemetery attendant's eyes twinkled. "Well, I was at home with my wife. She cooked me a fancy steak dinner to celebrate our fifteenth wedding anniversary. We spent the evening watching movies and chatting until midnight. Then we went to bed, and I got up at seven to get ready for work. Why?"

Charli glanced up from her notebook. "I'm afraid there's been an incident at the funeral home, and we need to confirm the whereabouts of everyone who had access to the building. Can we get your wife's contact information to confirm this?"

The joy fell from his face. "I'm so sorry to hear that. But, of course, I'll give you her number."

Matthew dialed the number and stepped away to speak with Mr. Stinett's wife. As he spoke with Mrs. Stinett on speakerphone, Charli overheard her share the same exact story as her husband had. She even offered to show the detectives the footage from their home security system to corroborate her husband's arrival and departure the next morning. It seemed Gary was in the clear.

Two employees down, only twenty-six to go. At this point, holding the logbook outside the crime scene sounded less boring than hearing about twenty-six ordinary evenings.

"Do you work much with the funeral home staff, Mr. Stinett?" Charli continued her conversation with Gary while her partner tried to wrangle himself off the phone. Gary's wife was telling him all about how *Forrest Gump* was the first movie she and her husband had ever watched together. By the sound of her upbeat voice, she and Gary were a match made in Chatty Cathy heaven.

"No, can't say I see any of them much except when I go to grab my tools. I hardly even see the other cemetery staff. It's only one of us per shift, so I'm out here on my own. Well... unless there's going to be a burial, then a couple other guys we keep on call come in to help. But it sure is good to have company this morning."

Charli forced a smile, but she was eager to extricate herself from the conversation. There was no time to be this man's "company" with the long list of people they had to contact.

As soon as Matthew hung up, Charli and Matthew excused themselves. "Thanks so much for your time, Mr. Stinett, but we've got a busy day ahead of us."

Gary flashed the detectives one last face-splitting grin. "Not a problem. You two have a good one now."

Matthew groaned once they reached the funeral home again. "This is going to be a fun day, huh?"

Charli leaned against the red brick wall. Though it was in the shade, it did little to cool her back. "Let's just get the owners' contact information from Mr. Cobb. Then we can start interviews with the employees who didn't show up. Let's hope the information they give us can guide our investigation."

Matthew flexed his right hand and grimaced. "That would be great. Because right now, this investigation is a ship lost at sea, and we don't even have a map."

Matthew wasn't wrong, but that was fine. Charli was confident they could still steer this ship back on course. They always did.

4

After Bernie Cobb had finished with his client meeting, Charli and Matthew asked him for the owners' contact information. He had appeared shaken by this, insisting that the owners would have nothing valuable to share with them.

Charli had gotten the vibe that the Kirklands did not like to be disturbed, and any time they were, the funeral director had to deal with their displeasure. Regardless, the detectives couldn't avoid calling the owners of the funeral home during their investigation. Mr. Cobb would have to deal with whatever attitude they sent his way.

After Charli had twisted his arm, the director provided their contact information and proceeded to take them around the funeral home. It was his way of showing how precise their procedure was.

"This is our embalming room." Bernie Cobb pulled out a handkerchief and mopped the sweat off his forehead with one hand while waving at a set of double doors with the other. "As you'll see, all our equipment is state-of-the-art."

Charli examined the director. In addition to sweating, his

face was cherry red. He'd been that way ever since she'd insisted he provide the funeral home owners' contact information.

"They don't even do anything here," he'd told her, coming very close to stuttering. "The both of them are likely on some island right now, sunning themselves into skin cancer while I keep shop."

Charli hadn't let him off that easily, just as she'd practically forced Cobb to be the one to give them this personal tour. She didn't quite know what to think of the man and wanted to watch him more closely.

With a groan, Matthew stepped into the embalming room. Tearing her gaze from Cobb, Charli followed, surprised to find a body on the table. Bernie hadn't thought to warn them that he was currently embalming a, um, guest. Though, why would he? They were detectives. Charli and Matthew had obviously seen their fair share of dead bodies.

Although, for Matthew, that part of the job never got any easier. He was squeamish every time they had to go to the medical examiner's office. Matthew always got through it, of course. It was part of his job.

Charli could only imagine how he was feeling now, though. Finally, they had a case without a brutally maimed body attached to it, and he still had to witness some gore. He probably wasn't thrilled about that.

And, in several ways, this was even worse than the medical examiner's office. The M.E. was only tasked with investigating the body to determine the cause of death. But a mortician was responsible for making sure the body looked presentable for the funeral.

That involved a lot of prepping. The room reeked of formaldehyde so severely that Charli thought she wouldn't get the smell out of her jacket for weeks. One of the major veins had been opened up so the blood could drain from the body.

It was utterly fascinating. To Charli, at least. Matthew was turning an interesting shade of green.

Brrraaapp.

An ungodly wave of flatulence emanated from the corpse, and Matthew jumped as if he'd been poked by a stick. "It's alive!"

Bernie chuckled. "Detective, I assure you, we're not embalming a zombie. This is a normal part of the process. Gas is often trapped in the gut and not released until after the deceased is on our table. We shift the body significantly, causing the gas to come out."

Matthew was staring at Cobb, wide-eyed. His head moved between Cobb and the body. "Y-you're sure about that?"

Charli stifled a laugh to maintain her professional appearance, though she wouldn't miss an opportunity to give Matthew a good teasing in the future.

Cobb made no effort to hide how funny this all was. He put his hand to his lips as he let out another laugh. "Yes, Detective. I'm positively sure that this body is not alive."

❄

Charli was still laughing an hour later as Matthew poked at his fries at the local diner. She was never going to let Matthew live that down.

Matthew sucked down his soda, and Charli pointed at it before gasping. "Your straw! I think I just saw it move! It's alive!"

Matthew rolled his eyes. "You think you're so funny…"

Charli popped a fry into her mouth. "You'd think after our last case, you'd be well aware that zombies aren't real."

"Maybe that's why I'm so easily startled. I didn't walk away from our last case unharmed, remember?" Matthew raised his bandaged arm.

His voice was teasing, but his words still caused a dagger of guilt to penetrate Charli's heart. The memory of Matthew being slashed in the arm was seared into her brain. For a moment there, she'd thought the knife was going into his neck. The mere thought of losing him choked her up, and Charli wasn't quick to cry.

But it would be like losing Madeline all over again. Madeline Ferguson had been her very best friend growing up, the only person she could trust. She had been Charli's boulder in the thunderstorm that was her life. And when Madeline was kidnapped and murdered, that storm raged so heavily that Charli almost drowned in it.

But she didn't. She'd learned to swim. And she'd dedicated her life to helping other victims like Madeline receive the justice they deserved. Justice Madeline had never attained.

As strong as she was, though, Charli didn't think she could go through that twice. Matthew was her best friend now, her partner in anti-crime. How dangerous this job could be was not lost on Charli. She told herself that she was there to protect Matthew, and she was. But their last case was a stark reminder that she couldn't always keep him out of harm's way.

"How's your arm feeling?" That question was all Charli could muster, even as she considered how deeply she needed Matthew. She never was good at articulating her feelings.

"It's fine. Still hurts, but Tylenol is helping."

"Tylenol is all the doctor gave you for it?"

Matthew gripped his burger with his left hand and lifted it to his mouth. "Nah, but I can't come to work on painkillers."

Charli was about to chastise him for being a workaholic, but she knew he would only point out her hypocrisy. She took a bite of her own burger instead.

They ate in silence for a few minutes, and Charli shifted her legs on the red leather diner booth. The restaurant looked straight out of the 1950s, with crimson barstools and metallic ridged walls. It was one of their favorite places to eat. Charli devoured their fries, and Matthew was a sucker for their strawberry milkshakes.

"So, Charli, what's our next move?"

"Well, I want to interview Jacob and Elwood, of course. We should find out why they didn't show up for work. Maybe Candace's place should be our next stop."

Charli was waiting on a warrant to get Candace's cell phone records. That would take at least a few hours.

Matthew ran a stubby fry through a mound of ketchup. "You think she'll be at home?"

"It's possible. Could be that she's just hungover at home. Or maybe she's in need of assistance." Charli wasn't hopeful of that, though.

Though Candace could have theoretically left through the back door without her car, it would have been a bold move to make in the wee hours of the morning. The funeral home wasn't in the best part of town. And if she'd been in trouble and wandering the roads late at night, wouldn't she have been noticed at some point?

But Charli didn't make assumptions. Sure, she considered every possibility, but she didn't believe in following her gut. She relied on fact and fact alone.

"Then let's go check on her." Matthew tossed his napkin on his plate before fishing in his wallet to leave cash on the table, since Charli had picked up the last bill. They didn't need a receipt. The partners ordered the same meal every time they came in and knew what it cost.

Candace lived in an apartment building near the square downtown. Though Charli had driven by the apartment building many times, she'd never had a reason to go in. From ads she'd seen in the paper, rent at these apartments was more than the mortgage on most houses. She wasn't friends with anyone rich enough to afford to live in them. How could Candace possibly afford such a ritzy apartment?

Charli pulled the car up next to the curb. "You ever been here?"

"Not even once."

"Leland Jackson Apartments" was plastered in bold gold lettering above the heavy French doors. The inner lobby looked more like a hotel than an apartment building. It even had what appeared to be a large circular concierge desk.

"Man, this place is gaudy." Matthew's gaze darted from the ornate cream and emerald rug to the white wainscoting that adorned the walls.

"No kidding. She lives on the third floor. Now we just need to find the staircase." Charli searched the lobby for a stairwell.

"Oh, the elevator is right at the end of the hall there!" A perky blonde woman stood from the chair at the circular desk. "Can I help you with anything?"

"Actually, yes." Charli pulled out her badge. "We're looking for Candace Redding's apartment. I'm Detective Cross, and this is Detective Church. We've come to do a welfare check."

The woman raised a hand to her chest, her eyes as wide as saucers. "Of course. She's in 306, but if you want to speak with her, I'm afraid she isn't home right now. I sure hope she's not in any kind of trouble."

Matthew tilted his head. "Do you know when all the residents are home?"

"Absolutely. We have a smart hub that connects to each

resident's phone. It's to automatically lock the doors in case they forget to. Not all the residents are connected to it, but Ms. Redding is. She's very careful about personal security." The woman's teeth were so bright, her smile could glow in the dark. With her silky hair parted to perfection, she was straight out of a *Home Living* magazine.

Matthew leaned against the desk. "Can you tell us anything else about Ms. Redding?"

The woman put a finger on her chin. "Is anything wrong with Ms. Redding? I'm really starting to worry."

Charli flashed the blonde a friendly smile. "We hope not, but any information you can provide us will be extremely helpful."

"Well, she works as a secretary at a funeral home in town. She's a quiet resident, never had any complaints, and she doesn't have people over often. She mostly keeps to herself. I've only spoken to her in passing."

"When was the last time you saw her?" Matthew studied the back of the desk, where a computer and a set of security monitors sat.

"I personally saw her yesterday morning leaving for work." The vivacious blonde's fingers clicked away on her keyboard. "Based on the smart hub logs, the last time she was in her apartment was a little after midnight this morning."

Matthew motioned to the screen. "We need to get access to this video footage to confirm that. And the smart hub records would help."

The woman's blue eyes grew so wide they were in danger of falling out of her head. "Of course. Is something wrong with Ms. Redding?"

"We're not at liberty to say." Charli kept her answer short and sweet. "We'd like access to her apartment."

The receptionist frowned. "I'm sorry, but do you have a warrant?"

They didn't, of course, and since it was pretty certain Candace wasn't in the building, they didn't have any basis for a welfare check after all.

"We'll just go upstairs and knock. We'll come back by to get that footage." Matthew straightened and turned to Charli. "To the elevator?"

"Yep." Though Charli didn't see much of a point now that they knew Candace wasn't home.

Once the elevator doors closed in on them, Charli spoke freely. "We know Candace was concerned about her own personal safety and that she kept her phone on her person. Hopefully, those cell records will give us insight into her location."

Matthew put a hand on the golden rail that protruded from the mirrored elevator wall. "What would cause someone to choose to live in a place like this?"

Charli shrugged. "I don't know. You've got money, and you want to waste it on over-the-top décor and smart hub security?"

"That's not what I mean, though. If you could afford a place like this, why would you be renting? I mean, surely Candace could afford to buy a house, right?"

"For the security that comes with living in a place like this? I mean, she's a secretary, so surely on her salary, she doesn't make a fortune. But if she has some sort of lucrative side gig…" The gears were turning in Charli's head.

Matthew rubbed his injured arm. "Or maybe a wealthy relative left her one hell of an inheritance."

The elevator doors opened with a light ding. The same carpet and wainscoting decorated the third floor. They were able to find Candace's apartment three doors down on the right side. Hers was a heavy black door with a half-moon window on the top. Charli hopped up to get a look inside.

"Easy there, kangaroo. I've got this." Matthew moved forward and was easily able to glance in.

Charli frowned. What she wouldn't give to be tall. "See anything?"

"Not much. I can see into her living room, but all the lights are off, and there doesn't appear to be any movement anywhere."

That jived with what the receptionist had told them. They needed to get that video feed, though, to verify nobody was in the residence. "Let's move along to Jacob or Elwood's place, then. I don't think there's anything else we're going to find out here until we secure a warrant."

Their visit did provide Charli with one vital piece of information. Candace was nowhere to be found.

5
———

Matthew's arm throbbed even though he'd barely done anything today. He'd just had a burger and walked around, allowing Charli to open all the doors for him. Who knew such light activity could increase his pain this much?

He just wasn't himself today. He couldn't decide if it was from the blood loss on their previous case or the call he'd made to his daughter Chelsea yesterday. Either way, his body was dragging along. It was the first time he'd been at work since he'd been stabbed and thought it would've been better to just stay home and rest. Matthew didn't love vegging out on the couch with HBO, but at least he'd be in less pain.

He couldn't do that to Charli, though. Not now. They had twenty-something employees left to interview. That was going to be hell, even with the both of them working the case. Matthew would not make her do it alone.

"Everything all right?" Charli didn't take her eyes off the road when she asked, the careful driver that she was.

Matthew thought he'd been doing a decent job of hiding his discomfort, but evidently not. "Yeah, I'm fine."

"Uh, yeah, you can't fool me. Is it your arm?"

Matthew let out a long sigh. "Well, that isn't helping."

"If you're in pain, I can drop you off at home, you know. I'll conduct some of these interviews and we can reconvene later."

The green trees of the downtown park whooshed outside Matthew's window. He leaned his head against the glass. "Really, it isn't that. I can handle the stitches just fine."

"So, what is it?"

Charli wasn't going to let up. And if Matthew was honest with himself, he kind of wanted to talk about it.

"Yesterday was Chelsea's fifteenth birthday. I called to see if she liked the gifts I sent. She didn't pick up, so I sent a text making sure she knew how proud I was of her and that I can't wait to see her. And she sent back a message telling me not to talk to her anymore."

"Ouch." Charli's lips tightened, but her eyes grew soft.

Matthew let out a long, slow sigh. "Yeah. You know, I've always been busy with work, but one thing I used to do was make sure I had her birthdays off. We'd go to the roller-skating rink or the bowling alley. I always got her a mint chocolate chip ice cream cake. That's her favorite. Now she's in high school, and I always imagined I'd be there for this time in her life, but her anger toward me is worse than ever. For the first time, I'm thinking I should throw in the towel."

Keeping one hand on the steering wheel and her eyes on the road, Charli gave her partner's arm a little squeeze. "Throw in the towel on what, fatherhood? I hate to break it to you, but you can't. It's a position you put yourself in for life."

Matthew knew that, of course. But how was he going to be a father to a daughter who wanted nothing to do with him?

"Evidently, she's filled that role with her mom's new

husband. I saw photos her mom posted online last night of the three of them going to a fancy five-star restaurant for her birthday. The kind of thing you can't afford on a detective's salary. She's got the dad she wants. Who am I to stop her?"

Charli pulled up to a red light. She turned to Matthew, empathy radiating from her gaze. "I know it's hard, but you can't give up. Chelsea may not think she wants a relationship with you right now, but I promise she will one day. There's going to be a time when she misses her father, and you just need to make sure you're there for that. It could be months or even years from now. But as long as you keep showing her you're going to be there, she'll turn to you eventually. Don't stop trying."

Matthew could hear it in her tone. This advice was coming from personal experience. He knew Charli and her dad had a tumultuous relationship that she'd been trying to rebuild over the past few years.

"Maybe you're right. It's just so hard to be the punching bag."

"But you can take it. And, hey, your daughter is fifteen. Even if you were living with her, you'd be the punching bag. Take my word for it."

Matthew chuckled. "Yeah, especially with my girl. She's got an attitude on her."

The light turned green, and Charli redirected her eyes to the road. "She's tough, like her father. Just don't lose hope. No matter how much attitude she throws your way, send her texts daily. Better yet, send her memes. Search for videos on TikTok. You've got to speak her language. Most teenagers these days don't like to talk on the phone."

Charli could be really sweet when she wasn't stressed out of her mind from her caseload. Sometimes, they got so busy with their work that Matthew forgot what an amazing friend she could be.

"Maybe you're right. I'll give it a try." Matthew had been so absorbed in thoughts of his daughter that he'd momentarily forgotten about the case. "Jacob Pernell's place should be right up here. Look for 1266." Matthew leaned forward to get a better look out the window and spotted the house just as the GPS chimed, indicating they had reached their destination. "Okay, pull over. It's this blue one right here."

The blue single-story home with white trim had all the blinds open and the lights turned on. A white Honda sat in the driveway. From the looks of it, someone was home.

But when Charli and Matthew knocked on the satin white front door, there was no answer. Charli proceeded to walk around the house and knock on every window. Still, nobody came to the door.

Charli put her hands on her hips. "Clearly, someone's in here."

But without a warrant, they had no authority to open the door themselves. If Jacob Pernell wanted to stay locked in his house, he was free to do that until Charli or Matthew could provide evidence of his involvement in a crime.

"Maybe whoever's inside isn't avoiding us. They could just have headphones on or something." Matthew didn't want to jump to the conclusion that Jacob was dodging them.

"We'll just have to swing by later and try again. But if we get ignored twice in one day, my alarm bells will be ringing, and I'll definitely want to do a welfare check." Charli took a step down the cement stairs of the porch but paused when a silver Range Rover pulled up. A stout woman with plastic grocery bags wrapped around her arms stepped out.

"Mrs. Pernell?" Matthew took a shot in the dark at her identity.

She stood up a little straighter upon realizing Charli and Matthew were before her. Prior to Matthew saying anything, her eyes had been fixed on the bags she was holding. "Yes? Who are you?"

"I'm Detective Church, and this is Detective Cross. We're looking to speak with Jacob Pernell."

Her eyes narrowed. "My husband isn't home right now." The answer was curt, and she offered no further explanation.

Charli slid her hands into her coat pockets. "May I ask where he is?"

The plump woman shifted her weight to one foot. "He's probably at work."

"He isn't, actually. He failed to show up for work today." Matthew searched her eyes for a flash of concern.

But there was none. The fact that her husband had failed to show up for his job didn't seem to bother her.

"Then he must be out golfing. Or he could be doing something else with a friend. I don't know. I don't have him on a leash." Mrs. Pernell brushed past the detectives, taking the steps to the porch two at a time.

Matthew glanced at the Honda in the driveway. "Is the Honda your husband's car?"

Mrs. Pernell turned around, her lower lip in between her teeth. "Yes, but sometimes Jacob carpools to work, and when he golfs, one of his friends usually picks him up."

This behavior was nonsensical. Matthew may not have been an excellent husband, but he was intimately aware of the dynamics of a marriage. There had been no time that he didn't know where his wife was when they'd been married. They were both familiar with one another's work schedules. If his ex had gone to the grocery store, she'd shoot him a text. If Matthew wanted to go out and have a drink, he'd be damn sure he ran it by his wife first.

And yet this woman had no clue where her husband was, but she wasn't bothered that he hadn't shown up for work? Anyone in their right mind would be at least a bit worried about the whereabouts of their spouse...especially when police showed up.

Unless she knew exactly where he was, and that happened to be in the house? Was she covering for Jacob? Matthew had a hunch that she was.

"Could you tell us where exactly Jacob likes to golf? Or what locations he might be spending time with friends?" Charli took a few steps forward and rested a hand against the porch railing.

A flash of irritation glinted across Mrs. Pernell's face as she set her grocery bags on a wicker table. "No. I don't think I have to. Do I?"

"You don't have to do anything, Mrs. Pernell, but this is a police investigation. We'd appreciate any cooperation." Charli kept her tone cool, not accusatory.

Mrs. Pernell shifted on her heel after swallowing hard. "I don't know where Jacob is. And if you'd like to speak to him, I ask that you call first. Please do not show up at my house again."

"We may have to come back if a judge grants us a warrant. But we don't want to have to do that." Matthew followed Charli's lead, keeping his voice light.

The woman fished her keys from her pocket as a small sigh escaped her. "You do what you must."

They were about to lose her. Her hand was on the glinting silver doorknob. Matthew had to make one last effort to get a reaction from her.

"Can you tell us about your husband's relationship with Candace Redding?"

Mrs. Pernell spun around to face the detectives. "Excuse me? My husband and Candace do not have a relationship. He has a relationship with one woman. That's me."

Despite the assertion, Mrs. Pernell didn't exude confidence.

Charli pushed a short fringe of hair behind her ear. "So, you do know who Ms. Redding is, then?"

The woman snatched her bags from the table. "Of course I do. I know she parades around a mortuary with garish red lips and heels so high she could strip her way up a twenty-foot redwood tree. And I wish she would, and then collapse back down it. I assure you, whatever that harlot is involved in, it has nothing to do with my husband. Good day."

The slam of the white door blew back a whoosh of air-conditioned wind that reached Matthew's face at the bottom of the steps.

Charli let out a sigh as they deliberated on the way to the car. "Well, I think we can say that Jacob is definitely avoiding us."

"And his wife certainly isn't a fan of Candace. Think there's anything to that? Maybe an affair?" Matthew once again let Charli pull his car door open for him, but he didn't make another joke about her chivalry.

Charli strode around the front of her car before opening the driver's side door. "We can't be sure. For all we know, she just hates Candace for being young and single. Some people are so jealous that the mere presence of the opposite sex around their partner sends them into a spiral. And Mrs. Pernell seems like the type to spiral easily."

"Where do you want to go from here?" Matthew eased his seat belt over his chest with his left arm.

"Let's touch base with the sergeant and make sure she's got Candace flagged on NamUs as a missing person of high risk. Then we need to speak to Elwood. And hope he actually answers the door."

6

It was already getting old, going to houses and walking away empty-handed. When Charli imagined interviewing twenty-eight employees, she wasn't accounting for some of them refusing to speak to the detectives. That was going to turn an already painstaking endeavor into an excruciating process.

"If we can't get ahold of Elwood, what's our plan?" Matthew leaned his head against the headrest, looking a little pale.

Charli adjusted the air-conditioning vent to blow more air on him and shifted her focus to the road. "We go down our very long list of employees. Eventually, someone is going to have to know something. Even if we can't see who comes and goes out of the back door of the mortuary, we know that someone had to have a key to the building. There was no sign of a break-in, so one of these employees could be involved. Have you gotten a call back from the Kirklands yet?"

"Nothing yet. Bernie's probably right about them sunning themselves on some tropical island right now. Must be nice."

Charli reflected on the travel packages she'd scrolled through just this morning. She was ready to finally schedule a vacation for herself, something she hadn't done during her entire career, but then this case popped up and reminded her exactly why she couldn't just run off to some island to relax. Savannah needed her. There were victims who needed her, and one of them was likely Candace Redding.

Over the speaker of the car, Charli's cell phone started to ring. Charli clicked a button on her steering wheel to answer it. "Detective Cross speaking."

"Oh, sorry, I thought I dialed Matthew's number." Detective Janice Piper's tart voice echoed in the car.

Charli shook her head. "Nope. You called me, but he's right here."

Charli knew damn well that Janice was aware of who she'd called. How could she accidentally dial the wrong number? This was just their colleague's way of fishing to know if Matthew could hear her, so she could proceed to ignore Charli as usual. Could their fellow detective get any more desperate?

"Oh, Matthew, hey! We got the warrants for Candace Redding's computer and cell phone. I've got her cell records."

The cell records Charli had ordered, not Matthew. Which was why Janice had to call Charli back. And still, she avoided speaking to Charli entirely. The woman was a menace.

But at the moment, Charli didn't care. She only wanted to know what those records showed.

Matthew leaned forward in his seat, lifting the seat belt from his injured arm. "And what did you find out?"

"Last ping on her cell was around one in the morning at the funeral home. After that, there's nothing. Her cell phone goes dark."

Candace's cell never left the building, which meant

Candace likely never left, either. Unless she had left her phone in the building.

"All right, thanks, Janice. Keep me posted with anything else you find." Matthew tapped his fingers against his thigh.

"Will do!"

Charli hung up. "I'm thinking she's probably one of the bodies in the cremator."

Matthew leaned back in his seat again, allowing the seat belt to rest against his arm. "Most likely. I don't see many other scenarios."

Charli racked her brain for all the possibilities. "She could have burned her cell phone on purpose. Maybe this was an elaborate scheme to fake her own death. If you never want to be seen again, that's one way."

This wasn't the most likely scenario, though. Even if Candace had a goal of disappearing, why were there two bodies? It would only take one to fake her own death. And there were easier ways to disappear. Even if Candace had run into some trouble, why not just skip town? With the kind of money she must have had to afford that apartment, she could run off to any place she wanted. So, the next question was, who might want Candace dead?

"We need to think of this case in terms of who would have had the motive to kill Candace Redding." Charli could have sworn her partner had just read her mind.

But it still begged the question, if Candace was one of the bodies, who was the other?

"We still haven't seen Jacob Pernell." Charli made a sharp left to turn onto Redwood Street. Elwood's place should be a few blocks down.

"True. What are you thinking?"

Charli drummed her fingers on the steering wheel. "His wife seemed awfully jealous. He and Candace could have been having an affair."

Matthew let out a snort of laughter. "So, Mrs. Pernell put both of them into the cremator? The woman isn't exactly in the best shape of her life. I don't think she could have forced two bodies into that machine. Even if they were already dead, it would be hard to haul them up herself."

And that was another angle they had to consider. Were the individuals dead prior to being put into the cremator? Or were they killed on-site?

On-site seemed unlikely, since the forensics team had found no other DNA at the funeral home. That could rule out any violent, bloody demises, unless the perpetrator had scoured the place after killing the victims. Although someone could have been strangled prior to being put into the cremator. If that was the case, there likely wouldn't be evidence left behind.

Or, in the absolute worst-case scenario, the bodies were still alive prior to being burned.

A shudder ran through Charli. During her last case, one of the victims had still been alive before being brutally maimed to death. That death would haunt Charli for the rest of her career. The gruesome deaths always did.

And it must be horrendously gruesome to be cremated alive. That cremator reached such a heat that the victim would be scorched to a crisp.

No, Charli wouldn't allow her mind to go there without more evidence. At the moment, whether or not the people were alive prior to going into the cremator was irrelevant. It was far more important to figure out who those people were.

And Mrs. Pernell killing both her husband and his potential lover without leaving any evidence behind certainly was unlikely. Then again, how many people could haul two bodies into a cremator by themselves?

"We also need to consider how likely it is that more than one individual played a part in this. There were two bodies in that cremator. And someone got these bodies into the funeral home undetected. That's a difficult feat for just one person."

Matthew didn't answer. He was too busy peering out the window. "Wait, is that the house?"

Charli glanced over to find a dilapidated orange home with paint peeling off the side. This wasn't the best neighborhood, but the home looked more run-down than the other houses in the area. Overgrown grass poked through the chain-link fence out front.

"Looks like it." It was a far cry from Candace's luxury apartment.

Which only raised more red flags. Theoretically, the salary of a secretary and member of the custodial staff shouldn't have been vastly different. So, why was Candace staying at the Ritz while Elwood's home showed he was one step away from the poverty line? Charli made a mental note to check on Candace's finances. Had a wealthy relative left her a hefty sum of cash?

When Charli opened her car door, the wave of heavy metal music rang through the front yard, causing the overgrown grass to vibrate. The white wooden door to the house hung open, allowing whatever song was playing to permeate the front yard.

"You'd think in a neighborhood like this, they'd keep the door shut." Matthew pushed his own car door closed with the bottom of his foot.

It became clear why they didn't keep it closed once Charli and Matthew approached. Hot air radiated from the entryway. They must not have had air-conditioning, and the humid Savannah air outside was somehow cooler than inside the house. It was a sauna in there. And though people claimed saunas were relaxing, Charli found them suffocating.

She rapped her knuckles against the decaying wood trim.

"Hello?" Charli didn't expect anyone to hear her over the music.

Matthew leaned against the old boards that made up the house's siding. "Great, another person refusing to come to the door."

Legally, they couldn't enter a house to follow up on a suspect of a criminal investigation, even with the door wide open. The detectives had to be invited in. But Elwood wasn't yet a suspect. He was just a man who hadn't shown up for work.

Charli checked her watch before turning to Matthew. "Elwood's missing and the door is wide open, so I think we can get away with calling this one a wellness check. We need to make sure he's all right."

"Sounds good to me."

Charli stepped through the doorway, doing her best to ignore the swamp-like air inside. The heavy metal music blared in her ears from the right side of the house, causing the walls to shake. A frame against the wall vibrated, threatening to fall to the floor. The farther down the hall she got, the worse the indoor conditions became. The earthy odor hit Charli in the face so hard she had to let out a soft cough.

Charli had never smoked weed herself, considering how seriously she took her education in college. She hadn't experienced the party years of her twenties as her peers had, but she'd run into enough marijuana during her time as a beat cop to know what it smelled like. What she didn't understand was why anyone would inhale heated smoke in this already sweltering house.

The smell led her and Matthew to a bedroom with an open door. A rainbow bohemian tapestry hung along the back wall. Cluttered walls were painted a bright yellow. The only pieces of furniture were a full-sized bed with an equally brightly colored blanket on top and a low wooden coffee table in front of it. On the bed sat a young woman with frizzy, unkempt brown hair. Her foot rested on the coffee table, a bottle of red nail polish in one hand and a joint in the other.

Because of the blaring music, she didn't even notice Charli and Matthew had come in. Instead, she was fixated on the brush strokes she was creating on her big toe.

"Excuse me." Charli waved a hand around so that even if she couldn't hear her, she'd see her.

The woman jumped back on the bed. "Who are you?" Her head whipped from Charli to Matthew, her red rimmed eyes full of fear.

"I'm Detective Cross, and this is my partner, Detective Church." Charli fought the urge to clamp her hands over her ears as she yelled over the music. "We would like to speak with you."

"Detectives?" She smashed the joint against the coffee table, as if putting it out might somehow hide the fact that it was weed.

"We don't care what you're smoking. We just want to know where we can find Elwood Sanders. What is your relationship to him?"

Even when Charli was a beat cop, she didn't enjoy busting people for marijuana. She got into this line of work to prevent harmful crime. Charli didn't believe there was anything particularly harmful about someone smoking a joint behind closed doors, though there were plenty of other officers on the force who felt differently.

Wariness was plastered on her face, but the young woman introduced herself. "I'm Heather Chelsham, his roommate. Or, at least, I was. Not sure if I still am."

"What does that mean?" Matthew walked over to the Bluetooth speaker sitting on the floor in the corner of the room and punched a button to cut the blaring music off.

Sweet, sweet silence.

"Yesterday, he gave me two months' rent in cash. He told me if he didn't come back by then, just to find a new roommate."

"Wait, so he just left?" Charli eyed Matthew, who gave her an equally suspicious look. "And he didn't say where he was going?"

The woman played with the belt on her flowing brown skirt. "Nope. I tried to ask. He didn't seem to want to disclose that, but he took most of his stuff. Just left the furniture."

So, Elwood got the hell out of dodge. He obviously had no intention of showing up to work today. But why?

"Do you know of any illicit activities Elwood took part in?" Charli clicked down on the back of her pen.

Heather's almond-colored eyes drifted again to the joint she'd put out on the table.

Charli sighed. "Again, we're not here regarding the marijuana. But was he ever involved with anything illegal, to your knowledge? Did you know him to be a violent person?"

Heather screwed her nail polish brush back into the bottle. "I have to be honest. I didn't know him that well. But no, he definitely didn't seem violent. He was kind of a doofus. He mostly liked to party too much, but besides that, he didn't get into trouble."

Beads of sweat were forming on Matthew's forehead. He brushed them away. "Do you know much about his work life?"

Heather set the nail polish bottle on the cluttered coffee table. "No. He sometimes complained that cleaning up a funeral home was pretty gross, but he didn't talk about it besides that."

"When was the last time you saw him?" It was vital that Charli be able to nail down the time he left.

The woman wiped an arm across her brow, grabbing a

clip from the hem of her flowy green shirt and pinning up her hair. "Around dinner time, so seven or something like that last night. I remember because the sun was setting when he packed up his room. Then he just left."

Charli drew in a stifled breath. At least the smoke from the joint was starting to dissipate. "Did Mr. Sanders ever mention his parents or any other family members?"

Heather pursed her lips together before slowly shaking her head. "I think he said one time that his parents were no longer living. If he had any other relatives he spoke to, he never told me about them."

This guy sounded more and more like a recluse. "Did he have a girlfriend or boyfriend? Any friends he hung out with?"

The woman shrugged. "I have no idea. He basically just went to work and played video games. He never invited anybody over, at least not while I was here."

"Thank you for your cooperation." Charli couldn't think of anything else to ask at this point. If Heather didn't know Elwood very well, she would not be able to provide meaningful details about his personal life.

Matthew handed her his card. "If you can think of any other information we should know about Ms. Chelsham, please give us a call."

"Yeah, sure. And I'll let you know if I hear from him. But I wouldn't count on it." Heather didn't even wait until they left the room before she reached for her lighter once again.

Once outside, Matthew flung his good arm into the air. "Holy hell! I never thought I'd be so glad to be out in the Savannah sun. Man, was it hot in there."

Charli was so fixated on getting down Heather's information that she hadn't noticed the sweat that had been sliding down her own temple. "Didn't smell amazing, either. Let's talk things over in the air-conditioning, please."

It took a moment for Charli's car to cool off enough to blow cold air. But when the icy air flowed through the vent, she thrust her face directly in front of it.

"So, we're thinking Elwood is our guy, right?" Matthew slid his own face in front of the far-right vent.

"What? I'm not thinking that." Charli made a concerted effort not to jump to those kinds of conclusions. Matthew wasn't always so careful.

"Oh, come on! The guy leaves town the night before two bodies are found in the cremator? That's suspicious."

"It's suspicious, sure. But it's a tiny piece of a large puzzle. I'm not saying Elwood isn't a suspect, but I'm not saying he is."

"Well, I'll say it then. We've found our guy. Now we just have to find his location."

At least that last bit Charli could agree with. "We definitely need to find him."

Even if Elwood wasn't the killer, all signs pointed to his involvement somehow.

7

"So, I've made a records request for Candace Redding, Bernie Cobb, Elwood Sanders, Jacob Pernell, and Wendy Worner. Hopefully, we'll get that information back soon." Charli glanced at her partner just as the traffic light turned green.

"Wendy Worner?" Matthew fiddled with his seat belt, which had twisted into an uncomfortable loop at his shoulder.

"She was working the evening shift the night it happened. I figured she should be high priority on our list of employees to speak with."

Charli and Matthew had already driven to the homes of two other employees without finding anything particularly useful. The detectives were trying their best to assess Candace's relationship with the other funeral home staff, but both employees claimed they didn't know anything about her personal life. But then the medical examiner had called Charli about his latest report, and they decided to pause the interviews to hear what he had to say.

Randal Soames was the best medical examiner in the

county, and Charli had contact with him on nearly all her cases. They'd established a casual friendship over the years. Nothing like the relationship she shared with Matthew, of course. But Charli appreciated the work Soames did and his wit. That man never ceased to make her laugh.

"Do you think Soames is going to have anything valuable for us?" Charli made a hard right on the wheel to turn into the parking lot.

"Well, he won't have DNA, obviously, but there were pieces of a cell phone in the cremator. Maybe he'll know if any of that data is useful."

It would be great to confirm that it was Candace's phone. The cell records showed where her phone was last seen, but having pieces of her actual device would be more solid evidence. And it supported the theory that Candace was in that cremator.

Maybe.

What a crazy case.

Soames was waiting for them in the lobby. Usually, at this point, Matthew would start with a tense walk to the examination room. But since there were no bodies back there for them to look over, his shoulders were uncharacteristically relaxed as they headed that way.

"So, I'm afraid I don't have as much information as I usually like to provide you with. Those cremators are excellent at doing their job. But I can assure you, there were two bodies within that cremator."

Charli had her notebook in hand, ready to jot down any information Soames could give her. "But how can we be sure? I mean, there are a lot of different body types with different weights. Couldn't the ashes inside just be from one very large person?"

Soames smiled. "You're always on the ball, Detective Cross. And I considered the same possibility. But there were enough skull fragments in the ashes to further confirm two people were cremated." With gloved hands, the M.E. carefully held up what appeared to be a piece of a human skull. "Unfortunately, the DNA extracted from the fragments was too degraded."

It wasn't unlike Soames to talk about bodies as if they were a car and he was a mechanic. In his line of work, a person had to be divorced from the humanity of the victims they studied.

Matthew put a hand under his chin as he ran through the scenarios. "And there's no way to tell the time that the ashes were created?"

"I'm afraid not. All we have is the timeline provided by the funeral home. I can say that, based on the parts we recovered, it looks like two cell phones were likely in the cremator. We cannot say that with certainty, though, and any identifying data is burned away."

Charli shut her notebook and put her pen in her pocket. "Honestly, I didn't have a lot of hope that you'd find anything identifying a victim. I wanted there to be some evidence outside the cremator, but since there's not, you can't work magic."

"Oh, but how much easier my cases would be if I could. If only." Soames clicked his tongue three times. "I don't envy you two on this, though. Are there any solid leads?"

"Hell, there aren't even solid bodies." Matthew shook his head and ran his fingers through his hair. "We're probably going to be back on the road now, interviewing one of the other twenty-eight employees."

Soames let out a low whistle. "Twenty-eight. Like I said, I'm not jealous."

Charli checked her watch. "How about we head back to the funeral home, since the evening shift should have arrived by now. Maybe we'll run into Wendy Worner."

It seemed like the best next step. They still needed to wait on records requests to come back, and Charli wanted to start the process on a warrant to search Jacob Pernell's house in case he was hiding out in his home.

Although this investigation likely wouldn't progress until they could talk to the key players at the funeral home, the evening shift was a good place to start.

8

"Well, you will be pleased to hear that I got in touch with the owners, and they will arrive in about thirty minutes." Bernie Cobb straightened his perfectly pressed suit jacket, looking an interesting mix of sick and satisfied.

After her partner never received a return phone call, Charli was surprised at the news. "That's fantastic. But in the meantime, we'd like to resume employee interviews."

"Be my guest. You know your way around by now." Cobb did an about-face as he rushed to return to his office.

Well, Cobb wasn't interested in speaking to them any further, though his rude behavior wasn't necessarily an admission of guilt. But like everyone else, he was on Charli's radar, so she made a note of his curt attitude.

A petite woman with straight black hair, wide eyes, and raised eyebrows stood behind the desk, her hands shuffling through paperwork. The papers slid through her hands with such force, it appeared that she was looking at one of those flipbooks with animated drawings inside.

"Wendy Worner?" Charli took a shot in the dark on this.

But since the woman was at the receptionist's desk, and it was the evening shift, it wasn't much of a stretch.

Wendy's head snapped up, the papers still in her hand. "Yes?"

"I'm Detective Cross, and this is my partner, Detective Church. We want to discuss the events of last night's shift."

The woman's green eyes widened even more, and if she'd been a deer in the middle of a road, she would have been hit by a car for sure. "What do you need to know? It was a pretty ordinary shift."

Matthew leaned against the desk and glanced at the papers, which she reflexively gripped to her chest. "Why don't you walk us through it?"

"Uh, well, I clocked in, and I sat at my desk. We had two different funeral services taking place, so I just smiled and nodded, answered questions. The usual stuff." Her words spilled out of her mouth like a waterfall.

Charli held up a hand. "Wait." She could barely keep up with what she was saying. The words were a jumbled heap of noises. "Did you see anyone go in or out of the crematorium?"

"No." The word was out of her mouth like a bullet. Wendy frowned and swallowed hard. "Sorry. I'm a little nervous. I just meant that, no, I didn't see anyone around there, but from where I sit, I don't normally see those doors."

Charli studied the woman. Was she hiding something? "Did you see Ms. Redding yesterday?"

Heat infused Wendy's face, angry red splotches popping up on her neck. "I-I...well, not exactly, but I did bump into her in the restroom sometime after I first arrived for my evening shift. You see, she normally leaves not long after I arrive, but she stayed a little bit later. She said she had to finish up a few things."

Why was Wendy so nervous? "Did you see Ms. Redding when she left work?"

Wendy shook her head vigorously. "No. I never saw her leave."

Charli jotted down a few lines in her notebook. "Can you tell us about Candace Redding's relationships with the other staff members?"

"Relationships? I don't think she's dating anyone, if that's what you mean. Though lord knows how flirty that woman can be." The receptionist let out a nervous laugh.

Matthew drummed on the desk with his fingers. "Does she ever flirt with Mr. Cobb?"

The woman actually blanched. "Not that I remember. But with just about every other guy that works here, yes. She's an attractive woman. Uh, I'm sorry, can you excuse me? I need to fax these papers right away."

"Please come back when you're done." Charli wasn't finished with this conversation yet. Wendy was jumpy, and Charli wanted to find out why.

As Wendy moved through the door to the back room, a head of fiery hair whooshed behind the back door. Whoever it was, they'd be their next interview subject.

Although Charli and Matthew stepped through the door only seconds after, Wendy seemed to disappear in a flash of light. Charli turned around to get another glimpse of the person with the red hair when a male voice interrupted.

"Are you guys looking for something?"

Charli smiled at the man. "We're looking for you, actually. What's your name?"

The redhead returned her smile. Charli guessed he was in his early thirties. "I'm Curtis Ricker, an intern here. Why do you ask?"

Another intern, so he likely didn't have keys, either. But Charli had to ask. "We're speaking with all of the funeral home employees regarding an incident that occurred. Do you have access to the building, Mr. Ricker?"

"Not on my own, no. I just come here for my scheduled intern hours."

Matthew stepped forward, his hands sliding into his pockets. "How long have you been working here?"

"About three months. I didn't work last night, if that's what you're here about. I actually just flew back from a family vacation this morning."

Charli checked for any signs of discomfort, but there weren't any that she could detect. "How familiar are you with Candace Redding?"

Curtis barely stifled a laugh. "Not as familiar as Bernie Cobb seems to be."

Charli caught his drift, but she needed specific answers. "Are you implying that Mr. Cobb and Ms. Redding have a romantic relationship?"

The redhead made no attempt to hide the smirk on his face. "I heard they used to hook up, yeah. I've never seen anything myself, obviously. I don't even work at the same time as Candace. Wendy's always here when I'm on. But I've seen her the few times I've switched shifts. A total fox of a woman, that one."

So, according to Wendy, Bernie and Candace had no relationship, but she flirted with everyone. Now, Curtis contradicted that. "Would you consider Ms. Redding particularly flirtatious? Did she have any other romantic relationships or friendships around the office?"

Curtis shrugged. "Like I said, I didn't work with the woman. I only know that she's hot, and that people say she was screwing Bernie."

Charli was forming the next question in her mind when Bernie stepped into the room. "Detectives, the owners have just arrived. You can speak to them in the lobby. Nobody else will be in there now that Wendy's gone home."

Matthew did a comic double take. "Excuse me, Ms. Worner left?"

"Yeah, said she had a stomachache. I told her she could go home as long as she had already spoken to you guys. She did speak with you, right?"

Matthew groaned. "Uh, sort of, but we weren't finished."

Charli exchanged a glance with her partner. Dammit, why were all these employees so elusive? Now hunting down Wendy would be a chore.

The director straightened his already perfect tie. "Well, the Kirklands are waiting for you in the lobby. And they do not like to be kept waiting for long."

As Bernie returned to his office, a snicker escaped Curtis's lips. He gave a quick shake of his head.

"What?" Charli cocked her head toward him. "Is something funny?"

"It's just…I know exactly what kind of stomachache she has."

Was he implying that Wendy was pregnant? "What do you mean?"

"Wendy likes to drink on the job." Curtis mimicked lifting a glass to his lips. "You didn't hear it from me, but I've seen her get behind the wheel drunk. The girl is a total mess."

That might account for her nervousness. Did Wendy have something to do with the dead bodies, or was she simply scared to reveal her drinking on the job?

Charli flashed the man a smile. "Thank you for taking the time to speak with us, Mr. Ricker."

The owners were of little help because they both had alibis. The couple had spent the evening at a fundraising gala.

Though how either of them got through a single evening together was beyond Charli's imagination.

The wife seemed just about ready to be rolled into a coffin herself. Large, gray bags sat underneath her nearly black eyes. The simple act of straightening her blouse was done in slow motion. If Mrs. Melinda Kirkland had a spirit animal, it was a sloth.

Until her husband, Lee, said something she disagreed with. At that point, the woman became all tiger.

"Bernie is on his last leg here. I swear it. I am this close to firing his ass! Do you know how many complaints we have about him on Yelp? And now there is a police investigation? People are supposed to arrive here already dead!" Charli could practically see the smoke rising from Lee Kirkland's ears.

Ironically, though they seemed to loathe each other, Mr. Kirkland and Mr. Cobb shared the same quick temper. They also shared a permanent wrinkle between their scrunched brows.

Mrs. Kirkland glared at her husband. "Bernie has been great to us! Remember when we were in the Bahamas, and we didn't hear a peep from the business? Not so long ago, I couldn't enjoy a single vacation back when you ran the shop."

"Oh, so now you're saying I'm more incompetent than Bernie?" The owner stiffened his jaw, the anger radiating off him in waves.

"You've got a fraction of that man's competency. Now, only if you had a fraction of his hairline." Melinda Kirkland's voice was a full octave higher than normal. Maybe her spirit animal was a chihuahua instead.

Mr. Kirkland's jaw dropped. "Yeah, maybe if I had his hair, I wouldn't have walked in on you and the cabana boy in Cabo."

Charli cleared her throat. "All right then, we've got a few more questions for you, if you don't mind." She didn't wait for a response. "Did either of you know Candace Redding?"

Mr. Kirkland tore his gaze away from his bickering wife. "Of course, I knew her. I hired her."

Melinda put her hands on her hips, her face puckering in a scowl. "You didn't hire her, Lee. Bernie did! You know he does everything around here."

The owner's eyes shot daggers at Mrs. Kirkland. "Bernie may have conducted the interview, but I'm the one who hired her, just like I'm the one who pays her salary."

Charli suppressed a smile. "And approximately how much is her salary, Mr. Kirkland?"

"Well," Mr. Kirkland rubbed a hand across his chin, "I have so many employees, so I can't tell you the exact figure off the top of my head, but it's around forty-five grand a year."

That made her gross monthly income around thirty-seven hundred dollars. Considering her rent was more than three grand a month, how in the world did Candace afford her luxurious apartment and fancy car? Charli flipped to a new page in her notebook.

Matthew flashed the Kirklands a polite smile. "When was the last time either of you saw Ms. Redding?"

The couple exchanged a glance, and Mrs. Kirkland shrugged. "I guess it's been a few months. We're so busy, you know."

Charli refrained from rolling her eyes. Busy sipping strawberry daiquiris under an oversized umbrella, maybe. She smiled at the married couple. "Thank you for your time, Mr. and Mrs. Kirkland. We'll contact you if we have any additional questions."

There was no reason for Matthew and Charli to stay and suffer through the couple's bickering any longer, although it was tempting. This was better than reality TV.

"Okay. Maybe we can swing by and see if Wendy is home.

And if not, we can—" A buzz from her pocket caught Charli off guard.

"What is it?" Matthew tried to peek at her phone screen.

"Oh, crap. I completely forgot…I have a date tonight. For drinks, not dinner."

A sheepish smile crawled onto Matthew's cheeks. "With that geeb agent, huh?"

Charli let her eyes roll to the heavens this time. "Yeah, that's the one."

Although the last night Charli spent with Preston Powell hadn't been so hot—not in her estimation, anyway—she'd agreed to get a drink with him. A part of her was considering a last-minute cancellation, but she wanted to give Preston a second chance. Perhaps they'd have better chemistry if they spent some time talking in a low-key atmosphere.

"We should probably end things for the night after you drop me off, anyway." Matthew shrugged. "We'll meet up in the morning. Enjoy your date. Be back before you turn into a pumpkin."

Charli gave him a friendly shove to his good arm. "Okay, Dad. I'll try."

9

Charli reached for the driver's side door when a deep voice rang out. "Detective, wait up!"

Matthew was already sitting in the passenger seat, so Charli knew Cobb must have been referring to her as he rushed over to her car. "Yes?"

"I just found this in Candace's office. I thought it may be of use to you." The words came out in short huffs.

He placed the black leather-bound book in her hand. A quick gust of air blew her short bangs back as she used her thumb to flip all the pages inside in a single motion. "What is this?"

"A notebook that belongs to Candace. I used to catch her writing in the thing all the time. I found it in the top drawer. Since it's not for work, I assume it's some kind of diary." His face grew red. "I didn't read anything."

Charli held up the notebook. "Thank you for this. Please, if you find any more of her belongings, let us know."

"I will." Cobb's answer was quick, and he turned on his heel to head back to the funeral home. The man scurried back in like a mouse chasing a piece of cheese.

Charli clutched the notebook as if she'd just been handed an ancient golden chalice with a secret code embedded inside. And she may as well have been. A victim's diary rarely ever included how they died unless the death was by suicide. But the pages could have plenty of information about the kind of life Candace led, which could set Charli and Matthew on the right path after so many interviews had failed to guide them.

Charli wanted nothing more than to grab some takeout and read over every page. But, alas, she'd agreed to see Powell, and it was far too late to cancel. And did she really want to? Was she willing to give the handsome agent a second chance?

Yes...maybe...

Either way, the journal would have to wait until after their date.

When Charli flashed Matthew the notebook and explained what it was, his face lit up like an evergreen on Christmas Eve. "This belonged to Candace?"

"Yep. Hopefully, it gives us some answers that we haven't been able to get from our interviews. Like, was she dating anyone? Did she have any conflict with other funeral home employees?"

Matthew traced his fingers along the journal's smooth leather cover. "Finally, a potential breakthrough in the case. I take it since you're going on a date, I can have this tonight? I'll bring it to you first thing in the morning."

Crap. That diary would be on Charli's mind every passing second until she finally got to read it.

After Charli dropped Matthew and the damn journal off at his place, she decided to head straight to the bar because she didn't have time to go home and change. She didn't look particularly nice in the outfit she'd put on this morning, but maybe that would work out in her favor. If Charli were to go home and get dressed to the nines, it might entice Powell to extend their evening together.

Hell, the man was already attracted to her when she was in khakis and a button-down white blouse. He'd be practically drooling if Charli were to show up in her slinky, midnight bodycon dress that hugged her in all the right places. That was her go-to outfit when she desperately needed a good lay.

But that would not be Preston, if their last encounter was any indicator. Why was she even agreeing to go on a second date with this man? If Charli had to provide a performance review for the night they spent together, only one word would be needed: lacking.

Attention to detail? Lacking.

Timeliness? Lacking.

Ability to satisfy? Lacking.

In all fairness, it wasn't all his fault. It had been late the night they'd hooked up. Preston had already been drinking, and Charli had been exhausted and worried. Prior to that night, she did have a genuine interest in the man. Maybe his performance had been a one-off? She was open to that possibility.

Her attire was fitting for the establishment he'd invited her to. Lowe's Pub was a small, casual bar in the heart of downtown. Charli had been here only once when Matthew dragged her out for a coworker's birthday party. Otherwise, she made it a rule not to frequent local bars.

Personally, she didn't think it was a great look for her as a detective to be buzzed in public. Though putting that aside, crowds and loud music weren't her favorite things.

Being a weeknight, only a smattering of people were seated at booths and tables across the bar. The music was a pleasant whisper in her ear, rather than the caterwaul she'd been expecting.

"Charli, hey!" Preston held an icy beer stein as he waved Charli over from a black leather booth on the right side of the bar. The Georgia Bureau of Investigation agent looked good in jeans and white button-down.

Charli found that she was actually happy to see him, and the smile on her face felt genuine. "Preston, lovely to see you."

He rose from the booth like the gentleman he was. "What are you drinking? Is IPA all right or would you prefer wine? Something stronger?"

Charli tucked the short hairs of her pixie cut behind her ears. She really needed a trim. "A pinot noir would be wonderful. Thanks."

Preston weaved through empty tables on his way to the bar top. Charli kept a steady eye on him out of habit. It wasn't that she didn't trust Preston in particular—she had no reason to be suspicious of him—but Charli didn't trust any man with her drink. During her time as a beat cop, she'd run into way too many cases where a young woman had been drugged without her knowledge. But Preston rushed back with her wine as soon as the bartender handed it to him, as Charli expected.

The handsome agent gave the glass to Charli, their fingers brushing as she drew her hand back. "Coming straight from work, huh?"

The glass chilled Charli's palm. "It's been a wild day. Unidentified bodies in a cremator at a local morgue."

Preston's eyes widened. "No shit. First time I've heard of anything like that."

"Same here. I'm not sure what to make of it. We can't identify the bodies, though we suspect at least one of them is the morgue's missing secretary. Matthew and I stopped by her bougie apartment to see if we could find her, but she's nowhere to be found. Her car was left in the lot of the funeral home."

Preston took a sip from his mug, and Charli followed suit. The fruity drink coated her tongue, the chilled liquid sliding down her throat like a gushing waterfall. It wasn't until that moment that Charli realized there was a bit of sweat on her underarms. It took a cool drink to remind her how sweltering it was outside.

Preston put his mug on the table. "No leads at all, huh?"

This was easier than Charli was expecting. She was no good at awkward small talk, but Charli could discuss her case all night long.

"None at all. We've got mixed accounts from other coworkers, so no clear idea of what kind of life this secretary led. Thankfully, and unfortunately, we've got over twenty employees to interview."

Preston's nose scrunched up, giving him a pained expression. "Ouch. Well, whenever I'm out of leads on a case, my mind tends to lean toward organized crime." He lifted an eyebrow. "Are you hungry? They make mean appetizers here."

Her stomach growled at the offer, and she took the small menu the agent handed her. "Actually, I'm starving." She spotted what she wanted right away. "Want to share a plate of loaded nachos?"

Preston grinned. "And some mozzarella sticks?"

Charli held up a fist and laughed when Preston bumped it. He went back to the bar to place their order and get himself a second beer since Charli had barely touched her drink.

When he returned, he told her about an organized crime case he'd recently heard about involving the son of a mobster who hid his victims in the trunks of crushed cars.

Charli shook her head. "Where?"

"Chicago."

Taking a sip of her wine and eyeing the door to the kitchen, Charli frowned. "I can see mobsters in Chicago, but Savannah? It doesn't fit."

Preston laughed. "I recall you thinking that voodoo priestesses didn't fit around here either."

He had a good point.

She lifted her glass and clinked it against his. "Touché, my friend, touché. What else can you tell me about OC?"

The field of organized crime had always fascinated Charli, and she leaned forward to learn more.

Preston flashed Charli a smile, one that reached all the way up to his eyes. She could get lost in those chocolate brown eyes if she wasn't careful. And although he wasn't nearly as tall as Matthew, his athletic build and sun-bronzed skin more than made up for what he lacked in height. He really was easy on the eyes.

"The average individual is ill-prepared to carry out a murder, even if they think they know what they're doing after watching a hundred episodes of *Forensic Files*." Their food arrived, and Preston waited until the server was gone and they'd both nearly scalded their tongues on the gooey cheese. "But they always end up leaving evidence behind. It takes a pro to walk away from a clean crime scene with no obvious motive."

Charli snagged a mozzarella stick, thinking about how she'd been leaning toward potential romantic motives for Candace's disappearance. After all, women were more than fifty percent likely to be murdered by someone they knew than a stranger.

But would, as Preston had stated, a person committing a crime of passion have been savvy enough to leave so little trace evidence? Was the lack of said evidence a finger pointing toward organized crime? And if so…why?

Charli considered all she'd learned about Candace as a person. "Our victim doesn't seem the type to be involved in organized crime. She's twenty-nine, and she lives in a very high-end luxury apartment."

Preston chewed another nacho before taking another sip of his beer. "A luxury apartment? On a secretary's salary?"

"Yeah." Charli loaded a chip with the perfect combination of meat, cheese, and peppers. "She had to have something going for her on the side or have been left a large sum of money."

Preston shrugged. "I don't know. That seems suspicious to me. Don't assume that anyone is too young or pretty to be involved in a criminal organization. If I were you, I'd go looking into her financials. Sure, if she's got a rich dad somewhere who is funding her lifestyle, I might be wrong. Or you might find a lot of suspicious cash deposits."

Charli stuffed the entire chip into her mouth. What was it Matthew had said earlier, exactly? Something about how if Candace could afford such a luxurious rental, why didn't she own her own home?

Well, she certainly wouldn't be able to buy a home without a legitimate source of income. Even if her parents were supplying her with this money, they'd have to co-sign on a home loan.

For the next hour or so, they sorted through all the possibilities. Preston shared tips on how to follow a paper trail, though he also advised she save herself a load of time and toss the project to a forensic accountant.

"Trust me on this." He broke the last mozzarella stick in half, handing her the larger piece. "That is a rabbit hole that you can get lost in for days or weeks."

As the conversation wound down, Charli finished the rest of her drink before fishing into her wallet for some cash. She was tempted to order a second wine, but she was driving and also needed to be up early in the morning. "Preston, you are a genius. I should consult with you more often."

"Uh, is that what this is?" He fidgeted with the edge of his shirt collar as she tossed twenty bucks on the table. "Just a consultation?"

Damn. She'd hurt his feelings.

"Oh, no, of course not. It's just that you've given me so much to think about, and I know my mind won't let me rest until I follow through on some of your suggestions. Do you understand?"

Preston furrowed his brow. He most certainly didn't understand, if looks were any indication. "I was hoping you might want to head back to my place."

That old, forced smile found its way back to Charli's cheeks. She was tempted, very tempted, but if she was going to sleep with him again, she didn't want her mind absorbed with a case.

"Uh, Preston, about the last time we met up. It was late. I was tired and in need of some…company. And it was great!" No, it wasn't, but it wouldn't help to say that. "But I normally like to take my dating life slower than that. I hope you understand."

Now, Charli had to discern whether the grin Preston was flashing was as forced as her own.

The agent cleared his throat. "Yeah, of course. I completely understand. Maybe you can give me a call when this case slows down a bit."

In an uncharacteristic motion, Charli put her hand on Preston's arm. "Definitely. I will absolutely do that."

Actually, Charli was torn, but she didn't have time to figure that out right now.

Charli could say one thing of Preston, though. He was a great detective. She was glad she'd agreed to come out tonight, for both his guidance and companionship. So, when he went in for a kiss, she let it linger for a moment before pulling away. It wasn't a total rejection, though not an invitation for any more physical contact.

She squeezed his fingers. "Talk soon."

Feeling his gaze on her back as she walked away, she was tempted to go back and take him up on his offer because, whether she wanted to admit it or not, she'd enjoyed herself.

Maybe too much.

※

CHARLI DIDN'T EVEN WAIT until she was home to check on the status of the warrant for Candace's financial records. Charli made the call from the road. They already had put out notifications to her credit card companies to inform them of recent purchases, but it would be useful to see her bank statements.

Once she walked in her front door, she tossed her blazer onto the coat rack that had been standing in the entryway for thirty years. On it, one of her grandmother's hats still sat. It was a hideous lime green with lilac flowers. Grandma had a soft spot for the seventies, even in her old age.

Charli could never bring herself to move the thing, even if the hat did look like a unicorn had vomited all over it. Her grandma's presence in the house made it feel like home. Charli may have lived alone, but with all her grandma's old furniture, she never felt alone.

Since it was still fairly early, she had every intention of calling Matthew to see if he'd finished with the diary. But when her hand was only an inch from the white receiver that hung on the kitchen wall, it began to ring.

The high-pitched jangle sent a shiver down Charli's spine. This phone never rang, not anymore. When someone wanted to get ahold of Charli, it was on her cell. Even her father, who had dialed the house phone for years, had relented to using Charli's cell after too many missed calls.

Ready to tell some spammer to take her off their call list, she picked up the phone and lifted it to her ear. "Hello?"

"Charlotte, it's me, dear. Marcia Ferguson."

Madeline's mother.

They hadn't spoken in several weeks, and before that, it had been years. Hearing her voice put a lump in Charli's chest. Guilt still plagued her like a shadow, constantly following her close behind. She'd stopped speaking to Madeline's mother after her funeral.

The woman had been a second mother to her, and after she lost her real daughter, Charli disappeared without a trace. Although Marcia didn't seem to hold it against her, Charli would hold those lost years against herself forever.

"Marcia, it's so good to hear from you."

And it was. Charli could hear flecks of Madeline's speech in her mother's voice. She was the last piece of Madeline that was still living.

"Oh, Charli." There was a heavy sigh from the other side of the line. "Maybe I shouldn't have called."

"What? No, of course you should have. What's going on?" With Charli's back pushed against the floral kitchen wallpaper, she slid to the floor and folded her legs. The curly phone wire wrapped around her forearm, a snake cutting off her circulation. Charli didn't mind. The position was reminiscent of her teenage phone calls to Madeline's house.

"Nothing really, it's just...I realized we're coming up on ten years since we lost Madeline."

Had it already been ten years? The fact stabbed Charli through the chest.

There was a time when she couldn't go a day without thinking about it, and now she hadn't even noticed that it had been nearly a full decade?

"I know. I'm so sorry, Marcia." Charli didn't want to admit the anniversary of her best friend's death had slipped her mind.

"I just can't believe it's been ten years, and we know nothing." There was a hitch in Marcia's voice. "All these years, and not even a bread crumb to tell us what happened except what you saw."

Charli swallowed hard. That ate at her too. It was one thing for a case to go unsolved, but another for it to go unsolved without even a guess at what happened. Even cold cases usually had a few leads that needed to be further explored.

Charli told herself she became a detective to make sure nobody else had to feel the anguish of an unsolved murder. But it was more than that. When she was just eighteen, studying criminology, there was a glimmering hope in her heart that she'd be the one to break Madeline's case. Every few months, for about seven years, Charli would do a deep dive on her friend's file.

But she never came up with anything that Madeline's detectives hadn't. And eventually, looking at the few details of Madeline's death that were known became too depressing.

Charli's stomach twisted. She shouldn't have given up on Madeline. But what else could she do? The case was a dead end at every turn.

"I'm so sorry, Marcia." It was all Charli could say.

She couldn't tell her that one day they'd have answers. Charli knew the statistics on ten-year-old cold cases. It wasn't likely they were ever going to know what happened. There was no real comfort Charli could provide.

A short sob came over the phone, followed by an unexpected laugh. "Do you remember when I took you girls to the ice cream parlor, and Madeline insisted she wanted pistachio, even though she'd never had it?"

Charli chuckled along with her. "Yes, I do. She saw this movie character eat it on a trip to Italy, and she got it in her head that it was a sophisticated flavor. You told her she wasn't going to like it, but she swore she was a young adult now who could make her own decisions."

In retrospect, that had been ridiculous, considering they were only twelve years old at the time. But try telling a twelve-year-old they're still a kid when they're on the verge of teenagedom.

"She spit it out so fast, the poor cashier had to mop up green gunk off the tile floor." Peals of laughter rang through the phone, and Charli joined in.

Charli had been wrong.

There was a comfort she was able to provide Marcia, even if she couldn't give answers. They spent the rest of the night with their ears glued to the phone, going back and forth with stories about Madeline. Some sad, some hilarious. The tears and laughter danced together until joy and anguish felt like one and the same.

At some point, Charli had stretched the phone cord far enough to grab herself a glass of wine. And then another. It was more than she'd normally drink, but it helped with the nagging memory of Madeline's disappearance. A few glasses of wine mixed with the one she'd had with Preston meant that, by the end of the call, Charli was predictably tipsy.

It was tempting to crash on the retro living room couch, but she was still in her work clothes, so she willed her legs to move up the stairs to change into a pair of pajamas. She staggered up the staircase, almost slipping on the sixth step, but she had her hand on the rail to catch her.

There wasn't a clean pair of matching pajamas, so Charli wore a shirt covered in palm trees and pajama pants decorated with navy polka dots.

Sitting on the edge of her bed, Charli glanced at her

pillow. It called her name, enticing her to lay her head down and collapse into a stupor. But the nightstand called her name too, and as tired as she was, Charli pulled the bronze handle forward and exposed an old, turquoise journal from her high school days.

In it held the last moments Charli had ever spent with Madeline. She'd documented every detail, even down to the daisies that were next to her untied shoe.

Each moment was burned into her brain, a charred memory from a distant past. But sometimes, she couldn't help rereading it. She even logged into N-DEx to go over all relevant files. Fire could harm, but it also provided warmth.

Charli only wished she could hold onto the glow of the embers without walking away burned.

10

"Are you looking for Candace?"

I looked up. A hunched old woman was staring at me. Man, I hated nosy neighbors.

"Nope." I slipped the hand that was about to reach out to Candace's doorknob back in my pocket.

"Oh. I was hoping you knew where she was. It's been a few days without sight of her. She's a sweet young gal." Her curly white hair bounced with each heavy step she took.

"I don't know a Candace, sorry." My shoulder brushed against her onyx fur coat as I moved past, pretending to be going to another apartment.

It was a rude enough gesture that she understood I was not interested in a conversation. When I heard the ding of the elevator doors closing and found the old woman gone, I hurried along the patterned carpet.

Key already in hand, I shuffled through Candace's door and slammed it behind me before any other intruding neighbor noticed my presence. Obnoxious rich people bullshit. The one thing I hated about moving into my own nice neighborhood was how rich people felt entitled to make other people's lives their business.

And because some snobby spoon-fed asshole would surely be watching Candace's place like a hawk, I had to do my search without a light on, which was going to make my night a lot harder. Why the hell hadn't I thought to ask Candace about any incriminating evidence she might have kept before I'd shoved her into the cremator? At least I lucked out when I found her apartment key in the side of her purse. Stupid girl.

I flipped on my phone's flashlight. The neighbors acting like they gave a shit about Candace was such a farce. They didn't. But now that she was missing, it would be the talk of the building. Everyone would gossip about what had happened with Candace, and it would be a race to see who could figure it out first. People with this much wealth were so divorced from real tragedy, they could make a game of it.

Though I couldn't pretend to be much different. Not that I was a rich snob, but I made tragedy my life's work. I'd accumulated my wealth with it. But I was still more down-to-earth than these bozos. I actually had to work for my cash. It wasn't handed to me from Daddy's trust fund.

Maneuvering Candace's place with a flashlight wasn't as difficult as I expected. She was an impeccably clean girl. Nobody knew organization like a secretary, I supposed.

I pulled open the circular golden knobs on her white kitchen drawers. The kitchen didn't seem like the place for a notebook, but people sometimes had junk drawers hiding out in here. Nope, not Candace. Her kitchen drawers were only full of kitchen utensils. There was no storage in her living room. Just open bookshelves, a glass coffee table, and pewter couches. White, sheer curtains gave a feminine, boho look to the scene. I thumbed through the books on the shelf to find a journal, but there were none. She clearly didn't read these books, either. The pages were perfectly aligned, as though they'd never even been opened.

Yeah, well, maybe it would've done her some damn good to pick up one of these books. If she'd had even the slightest bit of intelligence, she wouldn't have thought to test me. When that punk at the funeral home tipped me off that he'd seen Candace taking notes over the years, I'd almost come unglued. If the little prick had told me to begin with, I could have disposed of this problem a lot sooner.

And what the hell did she think she was doing with those journals? Was that a challenge? A threat to my operation? Oh, she jotted down the descriptions of a few bodies, and she thought it made her a criminal power player?

The girl had been out punting her coverage for years.

I shouldn't have messed with her to begin with. A little girl with big dreams. I knew the type. Really, I should have known better.

I proceeded to go through every single closet and drawer in her damn apartment, but there was no journal. I didn't even find so much as a diary. Which meant Candace probably didn't write down much of her personal life. She only wanted to keep a record of what I was up to.

Little bitch.

Creeeak.

I'd nearly given up when a walnut floorboard squealed under my foot. Nah, surely that girl wasn't handy enough for a false floorboard.

Wrong. I pulled the board back, revealing a large shoebox underneath. Hmm, maybe she was smarter than I gave her credit for.

Not smart enough, though.

The shoebox was bigger than normal. What had come in this thing, hiking boots? The box held a few loose valuable items. Gold jewelry, a passport, shit like that. Stuff I had no interest in. But at the very bottom were three notebooks. Bingo. Each journal was identical. Sleek, black, and leather-bound. I flipped one open and...what the hell?

No. Fucking. Way.

My photo was taped to the first page. And on the next few pages were more photos of my...*colleagues.*

I skimmed through the contents of each notebook, horror flooding through me. That bitch had written down every single detail of each body. She even had sketches. And how much she'd been paid for each job and what was done with the ashes.

These notebooks were a paper trail right back to me.

If anyone went into a missing persons database, they'd be able to piece together who had died and that the deaths were all linked. And man, were there a lot of them. And as for my picture? There might as well have been a neon sign flashing above it.

Even worse, for each person, there was a detailed description of who had brought in the body. My initials were even at the bottom of many of these entries.

I flipped to the back page of the newest journal, thinking I'd see the last man I'd killed before Candace. But he wasn't there. No, it was a redheaded bitch who made up the last page in this book.

Ah, I remembered this one vividly. It was the redhead with the fantastic body. But that had been...at the end of last year?

Then there had to be another notebook.

I hurled the shoebox against the wall, dropping to my knees to feel under the floorboard to find the other journal. Dammit, where was it?

Gone. It had to be in her car. Or maybe she'd left it in the funeral home. I couldn't say for sure. The one thing I knew for certain was the journal wasn't in this damn house. And without the fourth notebook, I was screwed.

I stomped all over every floorboard, just to make sure another false one wasn't hiding beneath my feet. But there wasn't.

Fury spiraling through my belly, I picked up the contents of the box and returned it to its hiding place. But I kept the journals. I would burn them tonight.

And I was going to get the last notebook, no matter what it cost me.

11

"That's it? The book is just descriptions and sketches of people?" Charli flipped through each page, unable to believe what she was seeing. This wasn't even remotely what she was hoping for. No entries about Candace's life? Not even a single page about her personal interests?

Matthew leaned over his partner's desk chair as she thumbed through the pages. "That's pretty much it. You think our victim liked to people watch?"

Charli dropped her chin onto her fist, thinking through the options. "It's gotta mean more than that. Who takes down descriptions of random passersby? And what's with the initials and dollar amounts? Are these payments of some sort?" She thumbed back a couple of pages and tapped an entry. "Three bullet wounds. Two to the chest, one to the head. Is she describing a mob hit? Maybe for a book she is going to write?"

Matthew patted Charli on the shoulder. "I have no idea. Sorry, Charli, I know you were hoping for more."

Charli drew her lower lip between her teeth. "I thought it

was going to be a normal diary, that she'd give us information about who she was dating or what she did in her free time."

Matthew shrugged. "Maybe this *is* what she liked to do in her free time."

"Take bizarre notes of people?"

Each page had a rough sketch and a detailed description of a different individual. It included their gender, the cut and color of their hair, what clothes they had on, and any identifying marks, including bullet wounds, bruises, and cuts. Under each description was a dollar amount and what appeared to be someone's initials—MD and NF.

That was it. There were no names, no indication of why she was writing this all down.

It was enough to make Charli want to punch a wall.

After a long, grief-fueled night, Charli could've used some good news. Charli had come in early, before Matthew arrived, and looked through the database of cases to see if she could discover any new ones similar to her best friend's. She came up short, as she usually did, and told herself to focus on her current case.

But now, the golden chalice of her current case was looking more like a dingy beer glass. She'd had high hopes of finding answers in this notebook, but now she only had more questions.

"I know this is a disappointment, but I do have some good news." A twinkle shone in Matthew's eye. "We've got the warrant to search Jacob Pernell's home."

Well, that was something. Charli shut the journal and tossed it on her desk. "Let's go over there now."

Once again, the house was lit up like a Christmas tree upon their arrival. There was something unsettling about every light in a home being turned on in the middle of the day. But at least it signaled to Charli someone was likely there.

Although, if someone was, they were silent as a church mouse. Matthew's knock reverberated on the door.

"Jacob Pernell? I'm Detective Church with the Savannah PD. We need to speak with you." Matthew's voice echoed through the open window by the entryway. The summer breeze whipped the sheer white curtains, forcing them to dance like old lovers.

Charli nodded toward the open window. "Think I could fit through?" It beat ramming the front door down.

Matthew bellowed a laugh. "You're kidding, right? A toddler could barely fit through that thing. Maybe if we can prop it open a little more…"

Matthew's left shoulder brushed Charli's as he moved past to grab the window frame. Grunting, his chest heaved upward as he used his full weight to thrust the window open. "Something must be blocking it."

"Whatever you say, Popeye." Charli leapt off the porch, skipping two steps and landing in dewy blades of grass.

Matthew continued to knock as Charli moved around the perimeter of the pristine home. The garage jutted out from the right side, out of view of the street. From where they parked, Charli hadn't seen the wide-open door.

A chill ran down her spine, causing her shoulders to involuntarily shake like a wet golden retriever. Something wasn't right here. The open window and garage, combined with the lights from the house, sent blaring sirens through Charli's brain.

"Matthew, get over here!" Charli moved into the garage, which was as immaculate as the outside of the home. Charli's own garage was filled with random cardboard boxes and old appliances. There was no cardboard in sight at this place, only white plastic bins labeled with neat writing and stacked on oak shelving.

"Wait, the garage door is open too?" Matthew's boots squelched against the silver epoxy floor.

"Let's see if this door is locked." Now that they had a warrant, there was no reason they couldn't enter the house. They'd announced themselves multiple times. Jacob may be in there hiding, but if he was, there was nowhere to go. He'd have to talk to them sooner or later.

Matthew had his hand on his holster, and Charli followed suit, hoping her partner didn't have to use his weapon with his only partially healed arm. Easing forward, Charli jiggled the door handle. It was unlocked, and Charli's weapon was at the ready. With Jacob refusing to speak with the police, they had to be prepared for any reaction, especially a dangerous one.

"Police!" Charli turned the knob slightly and then kicked the door forward, giving it enough momentum that she had full visibility of the hallway within a second.

The door ricocheting off the wall was the only sound. Charli turkey peeked down the hallway, but nobody was there.

After they cleared the house together, Charli suggested they separate to look for Pernell more closely. "You take downstairs, and I'll look for him on the second floor." Charli whipped her head back to Matthew, who nodded in agreement.

Charli searched in every closet, under each bed. She even flung open the cabinets in the master bath, though it seemed unlikely an adult could hide in there.

"I'm coming up!" Matthew's heavy footsteps thudded up the stairs. "You find anything?"

Charli met him at the top of the landing. Mahogany wood planks creaked under her feet with each step. "No, there's nothing. I don't get it. How can he not be home? He left the garage door open. Hell, curtains were swaying out of the window by his front door. Who would leave their home like this?"

Matthew let out a long huff. "Perhaps someone who had to leave in a big hurry?"

Charli nodded her agreement. "Could be making a run for it, like Elwood."

In the silent house, Charli's ringtone chimed out like an ambulance siren. She cursed under her breath as the sound caused her heart rate to skyrocket.

Get a grip.

Tapping the screen to put the call on speaker, Charli mouthed their boss's name to Matthew. He rolled his eyes.

"Detective Cross."

"I've got a treat for you." Ruth's voice had a singsong rhythm. It was a chipper tone that Charli almost never heard her use.

She lifted her shoulder, exchanging a glance with her partner. "Yeah?"

"Jacob Pernell is here to speak with you. Though he does have his lawyer with him."

The detectives tilted their heads at one another. "Are you serious? But we're at his home right now."

"Then get back to the precinct pronto. And brief me on what he has to say."

"Will do."

Matthew leaned against the banister of the staircase. "Guess he didn't leave town, huh?"

"Apparently not, but he lawyered up. If he's not guilty, he at least knows something about this case." It made no sense for him to get a lawyer if he didn't have some firsthand knowledge of what had happened to Candace.

Matthew shook his head. "I just don't get it. If he wasn't rushing out of town, why did he leave his house like this?"

Jacob may not have been running out of town, but he must have been running from something, and Charli couldn't wait to find out what that was.

12

Charli slid a bottle of water Jacob's way. "Thought you might be thirsty."

Jacob pressed his lips together, not quite a smile but not a frown, either. "Thank you."

Charli flipped to the next blank page in her notebook. "You know, we actually stopped by your house to speak with you, but it seems like you ran out of there pretty quick."

Jacob's lawyer, Tom Rawson, shifted his gaze from Charli to Matthew. "My client didn't run out of anything. He called me yesterday when his wife informed him you'd come by the house."

If that didn't point to guilty, Charli didn't know what did.

"Where is your wife today, Mr. Pernell?" Charli straightened out a wrinkle in her blazer, keeping her eye contact casual. She needed to know where his wife had been when they searched his home.

"She and my son are visiting family in—"

Before Jacob could finish his sentence, the salt-and-pepper-haired attorney leaned forward and held up his hand. He didn't want Jacob speaking.

So, they had to address questions to the lawyer. Matthew leaned forward, his button-down charcoal shirt creased on the corner of the table. "Why didn't your client just come out to speak to us?"

Mr. Rawson draped an arm over the back of his chair. "We're here, aren't we?"

Charli tried to shift gears and put her attention back on Jacob. "If you didn't leave quickly, why was your garage door open? There was also a window left open by your door."

A flush crept up Jacob's round face. "Perhaps my wife did that. She can be forgetful."

Charli rested her chin on her palm, feigning a casualness she didn't feel. "Is that right? Because when we spoke to her, she seemed to be anything but forgetful. She appeared to have a fine attention to detail. One of those details was that she didn't like the relationship you had with Candace Redding."

The lawyer jerked his graying head toward his client. No words left his mouth, but his eyes narrowed, and his message was clear. Jacob said nothing.

Matthew reclined back against the metal chair. "Can you tell us about your relationship with Ms. Redding?"

Mr. Rawson leaned toward his client again, whispering a brief message in his ear.

"We didn't have one. I did not know her well." Jacob's lips pressed together tightly, as though he had to physically keep himself from saying any more.

Charli tapped her pen against her notebook, the details she'd received thus far having been sparse. "Did you ever see Ms. Redding outside of work?"

Jacob glanced at his lawyer, who gave a slight shake of his head. "I have nothing to say about my relationship, or lack of relationship, with Candace Redding."

This was going to get them nowhere. His lawyer had

obviously coached him well. Whatever relationship he had with Candace, Jacob wanted to keep it a secret.

But why? In another situation, it might have been plausible for someone having an affair to lawyer up when a woman passed away. Even if they were innocent, being secretly tied together romantically would be a red flag.

In this case, though, Candace wasn't even pronounced dead. And while rumors might have been spinning around the funeral home, Jacob hadn't shown up to work. If he was uninvolved with the crime, how would he even know Candace's car was in the parking lot? That one of the deceased people in the cremator could possibly be her?

He shouldn't know anything, and he shouldn't have been motivated to seek legal counsel. The fact that he did was a clear sign that he was involved somehow, but was he a perpetrator or a witness?

Charli interrupted a hushed conversation between Jacob and his lawyer. "What can you tell us about Bernie Cobb? How would you describe his relationship with Ms. Redding?" Perhaps Pernell would be more open to talking about Candace's relationship with someone else.

Jacob shrugged his shoulders, as though he barely considered what his boss did outside of work. "I don't know about Bernie's personal life. He's my boss, and I do what he needs me to do. And if he had a relationship with Candace outside of work, I'm not aware of it."

"How often did you see Ms. Redding outside of work?" Charli reached into her pocket to pull out a folded-up piece of printed paper.

"I...I had no contact with her other than at the funeral home." Jacob sucked in a breath, his gaze darting to Mr. Rawson. The lawyer's face was unreadable.

"Then why did her cell records show multiple calls from

you?" Charli unfolded the paper, sliding it over to Jacob. His lawyer snatched it up first.

Candace's cell records had come in that morning, but they weren't extraordinarily helpful. Her last call was in the afternoon before she went missing, so there was nothing to place her at the crime scene. And while she did have calls from Jacob, she had also received calls from several other coworkers, including Bernie and Elwood. There was nothing that pointed to Jacob directly.

But he didn't need to know that.

He gazed at the paper in his lawyer's hand, and he fidgeted with the top button of his slightly too-tight shirt. "I only called Candace for work-related business. That's all those calls are."

Charli resisted the urge to roll her eyes. It might have been believable if Jacob wasn't about to twist his top button right off his shirt.

"Can you tell us about the last time you saw Ms. Redding?" Charli would take advantage of the heightened anxiety. Perhaps he'd be more likely to spill something.

Jacob tapped his fingers against the metal table. "I saw her a week ago. We don't normally work the same shift, but we had several bodies come in, and I had to stay late. But we barely spoke, and she seemed fine. Mostly, she kept to her office."

Even under duress, Jacob was able to keep things close to the chest. Charli and Matthew went back and forth for another thirty minutes with questions, but it was evident that Jacob was well-coached. The man was harder to break than fossilized rock.

The thing about fossilized rock, though, was that if one kept beating it until they hit the right spot, it would break open. Jacob knew something, and Charli would not give up. They just had to give him time to simmer.

Charli stood from her chair. "Well, Mr. Pernell, we'll likely have more questions for you later. But at this time, you're free to go."

Jacob's eyes grew wide, and he sucked in a sharp breath. He hesitated for a very long moment, his gaze fastened on Charli.

She studied him closely. "Are you okay?"

"Um…yeah…sure. Are you sure I'm not supposed to go to jail?"

What a strange question.

Charli lifted an eyebrow. "Do you think you're supposed to go to jail?"

Looking shaky, Jacob got to his feet. "Nah. I just know that a lot of innocent people end up in the slammer." A bead of sweat dripped down his temple as he exited the interrogation room, his lawyer in tow.

Before turning down the hallway, though, he glanced over his shoulder, staring at the detectives. Charli didn't want to make any assumptions, but his eyes seemed somehow…pleading? But pleading for what? For the detectives to leave him alone?

When the door shut behind them, Matthew leaned back in his chair. "Well, he was sure on edge, wasn't he?"

Charli couldn't deny that. "Definitely. But I'm sure he's got plenty to be nervous about. Even if he isn't involved, we're interrogating him. Let's not jump to conclusions."

But Matthew not only jumped to conclusions, he grabbed them by the horns. "Something is off about that guy. I'm telling you." Matthew rose from his seat.

Charli followed suit. "And if you're right, we'll find out about it soon enough."

Charli pulled on the heavy door, stopping when it was just a few inches open. Jacob's voice filtered through the air.

"But I did well, right?" The young man's voice was still shaky. "And you'll say that?"

Charli held up a hand, shushing Matthew when he started to speak.

"What the hell was that at the end?" His lawyer was as irritated as Jacob was desperate. "What were you thinking?"

"You know exactly what I was thinking!" Jacob's voice had grown a few octaves higher. "You know! And I did my part. You know it!"

A long sigh followed, but Charli couldn't make out who it belonged to, though it was definitely the lawyer who spoke next. "Just call me if they ask you to come back. You know the drill."

As much as Charli wanted to interrupt the little tête-à-tête, she doubted she would get any answers unless she could catch Jacob alone.

With the door still cracked, Charli could make out the clomp of their feet against the hallway tile. Her hand was as frozen as an icicle during a January snowstorm. She wasn't about to let either of them know she'd walked in on whatever they were discussing.

But what the hell had they been discussing?

She was dying to know, but not now. Later. She'd call Jacob tomorrow, when she felt sure he might be alone.

In the meantime, she still had a number of funeral home employees to contact as well as several other leads to follow up on.

Following the men out of the building, she watched them until they got into the lawyer's car and drove out of sight.

Yes, she would call on him tomorrow. Tomorrow would be soon enough.

13

It was a slow night at the Pernells' place. I'd know because I was the one nearly bored to tears as I watched him. You'd think for someone so scared of me, the man would keep his damn blinds shut. But no, I had to watch this man tuck his son under his covers, give his wife a kiss while she watched TV in bed, and then proceed to load the dishwasher with after-dinner dishes.

My eyes ached so badly, they pulsed inside my head. Staring through those binoculars all evening wasn't good for me, which was why I normally left jobs like these to other people.

This one, I had to do myself, though. It was too important. Tom Rawson had called, telling me that Jacob had made a mistake today when those cops had interviewed him, and he felt sure the detectives would have been able to break him if the attorney hadn't been around.

But taking the pussy out so soon after being questioned was a significant risk. This had to be done flawlessly, and I was the only one in this organization who was truly flawless.

Dusk was settling in, and an automated porch light came

on. The dimmed sky only made it easier to watch Jacob inside. But it also meant it was my usual dinnertime, and damn, I was eager to get this dealt with.

I leaned my head back onto my black leather headrest. As soon as it was dark enough, I'd sidle out into the yard and find my way into the house. My car was parked just a couple houses down, far enough to avoid being noticed, but close enough that my binoculars gave me a great view. It wouldn't be long now. The sun was settling in over the horizon, and the bottom of the sky glowed like embers on a dying fire.

Wouldn't be the last thing to die tonight.

I didn't want to have to kill Pernell because it only made things messier for me. But what choice did I have now? The man didn't know how to keep his mouth shut. He was so damn close, and he'd nearly said all the right things, according to his lawyer. I knew because I had that old bastard in my back pocket.

And according to the lawyer, Pernell was practically shaking like a scared chihuahua. What a way to alert the cops. I didn't need anyone sniffing around me like that, but Pernell wasn't a total idiot. He had to realize the implications of his actions.

Thankfully, the cops hadn't caught on. Even dumber than Jacob was, apparently. If they'd been paying attention, I wouldn't be able to waltz up to the front of his house and plant myself behind a tree right outside the back door.

I left my binoculars in the car. Being this close, I didn't need them. Instead, I brought Frank. My pistol and I were extremely close. One might say he was my best friend in this godforsaken world.

I watched, only feet away from Jacob, as he stuffed a coffee filter in the pot. Through the window, I could kill him right now. That wasn't ideal, though. The shattered glass would draw attention, and I'd have to rush out of here in a panic, which would defeat the entire point of my silencer.

Nah, I needed Jacob to come out here, but how could I make enough of a commotion to do that without attracting the attention of his family or a neighbor? With how terrified of me he was, a commotion might not even work. It might make him run to lock the doors.

Okay, I needed a benign distraction. I racked my brain for a way to get the little prick's attention.

I didn't end up needing a scenario because Jacob, the good husband that he was, pulled the bag from the garbage can in the kitchen. The dumbass was going to come right into my waiting arms. But from where? The door from the kitchen?

Nope, he walked past it. Would he go out the front door? I rounded the corner when I heard the garage door open. It was the perfect spot. His garage sat at the side of the house and wasn't visible from the street.

I ran around the house, arriving at the right side of the garage door just as it finished opening. Jacob's footsteps squeaked against his garage floor. The bag crinkled in his hands, and I knew he was getting closer.

And closer.

Just a bit farther now.

And there he was.

"Hey there, Jacob."

The bag dropped from his hands, crashing to the floor. Paper plates smeared with ketchup trickled out alongside an empty gallon of milk. Wild-eyed, Pernell scanned the garage, his gaze landing on me.

"I-I did what you asked. I c-called the lawyer. I didn't s-say anything." Jacob's dark hazel eyes snapped open so wide his lashes nearly touched his eyebrows.

I took a step forward. And then another. "Oh, I heard, I

heard. Don't worry. I'm just here to talk. But I wouldn't call out to anyone or anything because, you know, I do have my little buddy here. I don't want him to have to talk too." I slid the gun up, aligning it with his chest.

Jacob froze in place. Only his chest moved now, his lime green shirt rising in rapid succession.

It intrigued me, seeing people in their last moments. I always drifted to old memories of watching those old Discovery Channel animal documentaries. People were very primal in their final moments. Jacob reminded me of a wildebeest that just heard a crackling of grass nearby. The wildebeest didn't run, though every nerve in its body was on alert. It held out hope that the rustle of the leaves was just a meerkat, nothing to fear. Even when its instincts screeched that something was horribly wrong, hope won out.

And hope won out with Jacob too. He wasn't dumb enough to believe that I was going to walk away without harming him. But with his death imminent, just the tiny flicker of safety was enough to keep him standing there.

"W-what do you want?" His voice quivered.

I kept the weapon trained on his chest. "I want to know where Candace stored her notebook."

His hands trembled at his sides. How pathetic. "I d-don't know. I m-mean, she always carried it w-with her. She always l-locked her desk drawer, so that's my best g-guess."

If it was inside the funeral home, that would be doable. Better than in her car. The cops had already gotten to that. "Who would have access to those drawers?"

"J-just the other office employees. And Cobb, obviously. He h-has keys to everything." He ran a trembling hand through his hair. "Geez, you couldn't have found a different way to ask me about this?"

I let out a low rumble of a laugh. "I thought you knew me

well enough by now, Jacob. I don't like to make things harder for myself."

Jacob took a step back, his brows drawn together. "H-harder for you?"

I shrugged, keeping Frank trained on the little bastard. "Yeah. I mean, why not kill two birds with one stone?"

It only took a few seconds for his mental light bulb to come on.

"No, p-please, don't do this. I won't say a thing. I've got my family to think of. Please—"

I put the gun to his temple. In an instant, he sank to his knees, fat tears rolling down his cheeks.

He lifted his head, his eyes pleading with me in his last moments.

A slow smile spread across my face. "It was a pleasure doing business with you."

I squeezed the trigger. Someone was going to have a mess to clean up.

14

Charli was still wiping sleep from her eyes when she pulled up to the Pernell house at a little after five the next morning. She'd barely been asleep for a few hours before Ruth's call woke her up. Matthew didn't seem much more awake than Charli felt.

"You ready for this?" Matthew unbuckled his seat belt.

"Sure am."

Ready as she'd ever be, though she couldn't pretend this hadn't thrown her. This wasn't the kind of break in her case Charli was expecting, and it certainly wasn't the break she'd been hoping for.

The crime scene tape was still being rolled out by two beat cops. Jacob's wife was around the corner from the scene in the front yard speaking to an officer, if one could call hyperventilating speaking. She wasn't recognizable in her floral printed robe, her hair in a messy bun, eyes puffy above tear-streaked cheeks. A far cry from the pristinely put-together woman who had carried in her groceries in front of the detectives not so long ago.

"It makes no sense! I just saw him! I just saw him a few hours ago! There was no noise!" The screech in her voice penetrated the depths of Charli's soul.

She'd heard that voice so many times before, in other victims' family members, but it never got any easier. The sound echoed her own cry the day she watched Madeline get pulled away by the person who murdered her.

Charli straightened her posture, pulling her lips tight. She couldn't allow her own emotions to bubble up every time she heard a loved one in agony. Getting emotional wouldn't help the situation, and it only made her job harder.

"Mrs. Pernell, may we speak to you?" Matthew gave the woman a sympathetic smile as the officer nodded at the detectives and walked away.

Her eyes were glassy, her lips parted. An almost imperceptible shake intensified as Charli approached. The bereaved woman wrapped her arms around her middle. "I don't understand why this happened."

Charli reached out a hand. "Mrs. Pernell, we are truly sorry for your loss."

Sobs racked her body, and she latched onto Charli's hand like a woman drowning in the ocean.

"Mrs. Pernell, why don't we go into your living room? You can take a minute to take a breath and get away from prying eyes." Charli glared toward the lookie-loos already gathering on the sidewalk.

"You think I care? My son just lost his father!" All the color had been sucked from her face. Shattered to her core, she swiped a floral sleeve across her face.

Matthew scanned the front lawn. "Where is your son?"

"Our neighbors took him for the night when the police arrived." Mrs. Pernell's gaze fell to her wedding ring, and the sobs began again. "I just don't understand. How could he have been shot? He kissed me goodnight and said he was going to clean up downstairs. I was in bed watching TV while I waited for him to come back, but he never came back. I never heard a peep."

Matthew cocked his head. "Wait, are you saying you never heard the gunshot?"

Charli was as lost as Matthew on this one. In fact, she'd assumed the gunshot was how Mrs. Pernell was alerted to her husband's death.

"No! I heard nothing except the TV. I was watching one of my favorite shows. Maybe if I hadn't had the volume up so loud…"

Charli's heart clinched for the poor woman. She pulled out her notebook. "Mrs. Pernell, can you take us back to the last moment you saw your husband?"

"I was watching TV in the bed. I had reached for my glasses on the nightstand when I felt his lips on my cheek. Jacob said he was going down to do the dishes, as he often does after I cook dinner. I was so absorbed in the show, and I didn't hear anything other than the TV. I must have fallen asleep. When I woke up, I looked up at the clock to find it was morning, and it didn't look like Jacob had come to bed. I went downstairs to look for him and…" Mrs. Pernell sucked in two quick breaths. "I found him in the garage. Do you think if I hadn't fallen asleep, I could have saved him?"

Charli didn't need to see the body to have this answer. She'd already been told Jacob had been shot in the temple at point-blank range. "Ma'am, you did everything you could. This was not an injury you could have saved him from."

"Oh, god. My sweet Jacob. Who would do this? Who would take him from his family like this?"

Was this grief-stricken woman the same person who had given Charli and Matthew the cold shoulder before? She sure hadn't seemed to care about her husband then, unless it was an act and she'd known exactly where Jacob had been.

Charli shifted her feet on the front lawn. There was always a lingering discomfort when she had to question someone in this much distress, but it had to be done. "That is something we wanted to ask you. Do you know of anyone who would want to hurt Jacob?"

Mrs. Pernell swiped at a tear running down her cheek. "No. Jacob was a good man. I mean, he wasn't perfect. He made mistakes, but none that were worth killing him over."

"I'm so sorry we're having to ask you questions right now, but the sooner we do, the sooner we can find out who did this to your husband." Matthew flashed the grieving woman a sympathetic smile. "Candace Redding was reported missing yesterday, and now this tragedy has happened to your family. We can't help but wonder if there is some sort of a connection."

Mrs. Pernell raised a hand to her throat, her eyes growing wide. "Do you...do you think *she* had something to do with my husband's...with what happened to my husband?"

Matthew lifted a shoulder. "That's a possibility, but we don't have an answer for—"

A sob escaped Mrs. Pernell's throat, and she lifted a hand to wipe the tears rolling down her face. "Can you leave me be now, please? I need to go to my son."

This was as good of a place as any to end the conversation. They hadn't gotten all the information they needed, but their distraught witness wouldn't be helpful to their investigation at the moment.

"Of course, Mrs. Pernell. And like Detective Church mentioned, we realize this is incredibly difficult for you, but we just want to find out who's responsible for your husband's death. Tomorrow, we'll be in touch for a more formal interview." Charli motioned for a nearby officer. "Officer Hendrix will escort you to your neighbor's house."

Charli couldn't fathom the stress the woman must have been feeling in this moment. Sure, she'd experienced Madeline's kidnapping, but having her husband shot at her own house was unimaginable.

"No. I can get there just f-fine." A shakiness remained in her voice, but her tone was firm.

They'd upset her, and she was making that clear, but these questions couldn't be avoided, as offensive as they may have seemed to her. If there was an affair or any other type of relationship with Candace, it was vital to the case.

Charli and Matthew proceeded to sign the logbook and don their gloves and booties before making their way to the garage. Matthew's gaze darted toward the body and then quickly away from the pool of blood as Charli knelt down a foot from the victim to get a closer look. The crimson pool that encircled Jacob stained his lime green t-shirt. The right side of his face was unidentifiable.

Charli could put a few degrees of separation between her and the deceased. Despite the fact that she'd spoken to this man just yesterday, she was not gripped with sorrow. Frankly, it was harder to deal with anguished family members than dead bodies. Once she got onto the scene, she went into analytical mode. She had to be a robot examining dead victims. Without this skill, it would be difficult to do her job, to say the least.

A forensic photographer flashed a photo, and Charli squinted her eyes in the harsh light. "Have we found any identifying information? Fingerprints left behind?"

Another member of the forensics team spoke up. "Not yet. There was no weapon. The M.E. hasn't arrived yet, but I feel safe to say that this was definitely a point-blank range shot, so I doubt the perpetrator had reason to touch the victim. But we're still doing our search of the body, home, and premises."

"Time of death?"

The tech shook his head. "He's in rigor, but you'll have to wait for the M.E. to know more."

Charli took a step back toward Matthew, who seemed eager to make eye contact with her instead of the gore before him. "His wife doesn't seem to think there was anyone out to get him, but Jacob did."

She nodded, her mind drifting back to their last moments with Jacob. Charli internally kicked herself for not putting the pieces together sooner. She'd viewed Jacob's pleading as misplaced guilt, but had he really been in fear for his own life? If he'd just told her or clued her in better, she would have had a squad car out here guarding the premises.

Instead, she'd thought tomorrow would be soon enough. Well, this was tomorrow, and look where that delay had gotten them.

It wouldn't do to cry over spilled milk, though. This was done. Without a time machine, Charli couldn't fix this mistake, but she could utilize this information moving forward.

Charli bit her lip. "If he knew someone was coming for him, then it had to be someone he was acquainted with."

Matthew closed his eyes for a moment, running through their list of suspects. "Elwood told his roommate he was getting out of dodge, but that doesn't mean it was the truth. Maybe he's still in town."

That was a definite possibility. "Or maybe Bernie had a reason to get rid of Jacob." Bernie Cobb could not be ruled out. After all, he did run the mortuary.

Matthew's eyes snapped open. "Yes! That would make sense, considering we heard rumors of Candace seeing both Bernie and Jacob. Perhaps this was a revenge move for

Bernie on behalf of Candace. Or it could have been spurred by jealousy, or—"

"No. I don't think this is romantic." Charli couldn't get Preston's words out of her head. The man may be a lousy lay, but he was an outstanding detective.

Charli scrolled to her email to see if those records had arrived. They had. Tapping the screen, she opened the doc, scrolling to deposits.

Bingo.

"Matt, look at this."

He took the device from her hand. "Cash deposits. You thinking what I'm thinking?"

Charli wanted to think exactly what she knew her partner was thinking, but she couldn't get tunnel vision. "Yeah. She was getting cash from somewhere. I don't think it was a boyfriend, though, and we haven't seen any sign of her owning her own business or anything like that." Charli waved her hands in circles in front of the open garage. "I mean, look at this house."

Matthew furrowed his brow. "Uh, I'm looking at it, but I don't follow."

"Jacob wasn't making much more than fifty grand. Since his wife doesn't work, how could they afford a house like this? Who was giving Candace piles of cash? Someone with money is spearheading this crime. I bet running the busiest funeral home in Savannah, Bernie Cobb is paid handsomely."

Matthew rubbed his still-healing arm. "Would he be, though? I mean, he doesn't own the place. He's just middle management."

Charli let out a sigh. "Perhaps you're right. Or maybe, being that the owners are so notoriously uninvolved in their own business, he's found ways to skim off the top of the profits for himself." That would explain why Bernie was adamant the owners not be contacted. He probably didn't want them checking in on the funeral home, lest they discover inaccuracies on the books.

Matthew snapped his fingers. "Charli, I think you're onto something here."

Charli flashed him a grin. "I usually am."

15

Matthew peeked into the garage, attempting to be unobtrusive as the forensics team did their work. But he was more than a little eager to find out if anything new had come up.

It was going on nine in the morning. Charli and Matthew had assisted local police officers going house to house, trying to find out if anyone had security system footage they could access. Shockingly, only a few of the neighbors did, but none of the footage gave them a clue as to who had murdered Jacob Pernell.

In a neighborhood as affluent as this, Matthew expected a lot more of the neighbors to have security cameras. Evidently, they felt pretty safe out here. At least, they had. Matthew suspected that was about to change. Some were probably putting in orders for security systems as he stood there.

Additionally, they questioned everyone about what they'd seen or heard, which was a whole lot of nothing. At first, Matthew speculated that Mrs. Pernell had blocked out the sound of the gunshot. It wasn't unusual for victims of traumatic events to lose pieces of their memory. Or perhaps she had heard it but had been too deeply asleep.

Back when Matthew was a beat cop, he had to deal with endless calls about fireworks from people who assumed they were fired shots. People mixed up sounds all the time, and it wasn't impossible to believe a victim would mistake a gunshot for an ordinary noise and forget all about it after the trauma of finding their husband in a pool of blood.

But it was impossible that every single neighbor also failed to hear the shot. Charli and Matthew agreed there must have been a silencer on the gun, which would have muted the sound considerably. If this was the case, their perpetrator likely knew exactly what they were doing, which explained why there was no evidence at the scene of the crime.

Matthew only hoped that wasn't the case at Jacob Pernell's house. Hopefully, this criminal wasn't as much of an expert as they initially appeared to be.

"So, anything? A shoe print? Fingerprints?" Matthew gave a wide berth around the crime scene tape and walked across the silver epoxy garage floor, glad the body had already been removed. The floor shined like a mirror, reflecting Matthew's tired eyes back at him. It seemed unlikely that with a floor like this, prints wouldn't be left behind.

The member of the forensics team sighed. "Nothing at all. The perp had to be wearing personal protective equipment."

"Of course they were." Matthew flashed himself a furrowed look in the floor's finish. Were the bags under his eyes actually engulfing the entirety of his face, or was the floor warping them? Surely he didn't look that old. Man, beauty sleep was no joke.

"We're doing our best, but this is a clean scene. Whoever you're dealing with, they know what they're doing."

Did that further point to Bernie? The man worked at a

funeral home. It wasn't dissimilar to the type of work Soames did as a medical examiner. He could have had the expertise to pull off an unscathed crime scene, both at the funeral home and at Jacob's house.

But what was the motive?

"Any word from Cyber about his phone?"

"No, but they've likely got the report by now."

Matthew nodded to the forensics tech as he bagged his booties and gloves.

It was time to pay the cyber guys a visit.

❄

IN THE LAB, Matthew groaned and rubbed the small of his back as he pored over the printout of Jacob Pernell's internet search logs. Charli had stepped out to get them some coffee from the breakroom, but he really wished she'd bring back a giant sandwich. He was starving. It was after six in the evening, and he'd only had a pack of crackers for lunch.

"Bingo!"

Matthew glanced up in time to see a cyber tech fist pump the air. "You get it?"

The tech's smile told a story of its own. "Sure did. I did a combination of some of the passwords the wife thought it might be and broke it open."

Matthew could have cried with happiness. "That's great news."

He started to stand up, but the tech waved him down. "Give me a few minutes to clone the device, then I'll turn the clone over to you."

Rubbing his sore arm, Matthew leaned back in his seat, closing his tired eyes. If he'd been a praying man, he would have prayed that there would be a text message or voice mail that pointed a big bright spotlight on their killer. Unfortunately, Matthew knew things like that never happened.

It seemed unlikely a murderer as flawless as this one would give Jacob a heads-up phone call, but a man could hope.

"Here you go."

Opening his eyes, Matthew took the cloned device and thanked the tech before getting familiar with the screen. There were no recent calls, the latest one being two days ago from Jacob's wife. But there was a text received an hour before his death...from Bernie Cobb.

Did I not make myself extremely clear about what our procedure is? I expect better than this!

There was no preceding text message thread, which made no sense, considering Bernie was Jacob's boss. Surely, they would have other texts to each other. Jacob must have cleared their history, which wasn't routine behavior. Matthew still had texts on his smartphone from 2012. Those things didn't disappear on their own, so why would he delete them?

Perhaps because the messages at some point mentioned Candace, and Jacob didn't want his wife to see? Or because Charli was right, and there was something criminal going on at the funeral home that Jacob didn't want on record?

And why was Cobb so infuriated with Jacob? It didn't bode well for the director as a potential suspect. Though, again, Matthew doubted a man who was capable of such forensic expertise would send a text prior to a planned murder unless, being Jacob's boss, Cobb thought the message would seem routine.

There weren't any other recent messages, except a grocery list from his wife. An unusual pang stabbed into Matthew's chest upon reading it. Memories of Judy sending him grocery lists flashed through his mind. He had to take a deep breath at the recollection.

Matthew knew he was pretty much over his ex-wife, but divorce was funny like that. Even after all the time that had passed, a memory could hit him in the gut. More than anything, Matthew craved what he had when he was still married. He missed seeing Chelsea every night. He missed family holidays. He missed a warm, full house to come home to rather than his lonely apartment.

Matthew shook it off and continued to look through the phone. Movement from the doorway caught the corner of his eye. Charli handed him an ice-cold bottle of soda. "You're an angel."

Charli gave him a wry grin. "The coffee in the bottom of the pot looked like something you'd find in a sewer, so I hit up the vending machine." She twisted the lid off her own bottle and took a long gulp. "Find anything useful?"

Matthew rolled his head from side to side, stretching the muscles in his neck. "Nothing yet. The only thing suspicious so far is an angry text message from Bernie Cobb."

Charli screwed the lid back on her soda. "Funny you should say that. I was going to suggest that we need to pay a visit with Cobb." She glanced at her watch, looking as exhausted as he felt.

Matthew's stomach growled. "Can we pick up a sandwich on the way?"

Charli raised a fist to him, and he bumped, exhausted to his core. "I'll even buy."

Matthew didn't tell her that it was her turn anyway. "I'm going to put out a statewide APB on Elwood too. If this man is alive, we need to speak to him."

Matthew knew that Elwood could be deceased as well. He might have been the other body in the cremator. Perhaps he planned to run out of town but was caught before he could.

If that was the case, Jacob and Elwood might have been spooked by the same person.

"Perfect. Let me finish up a few things too. I'll meet you at my car in ten minutes."

As tired as he was, Matthew was glad that he wasn't going back to his apartment right away. It was times like these when Matthew wished he had the energy of his youth. Back then, he could work sixteen-hour days without breaking a sweat. If he could do that now, it would mean that he wouldn't have to return to the wrinkled bed sheets waiting for him at home.

When he was married, he used to see his bed as a refuge from the rest of the world. A place where he could relax his mind. Now, it was just a reminder of his loneliness.

But that loneliness could wait for another couple hours. They'd visit Cobb first and determine if the creepy funeral home director was also a murderer or not.

16

Charli pulled up to Kirkland Funeral Home just in time to find Bernie Cobb walking to his car. She hadn't known if he would be at work or at his house, but since the funeral home was closer, she'd tried it first.

Bingo.

He was standing beside his vehicle, keys in hand. The man looked as put together as usual and didn't look worse for wear for having killed a couple people in the past few days.

Charli glanced at her reflection in the mirror, making sure she didn't have mustard or ketchup on her mouth before stepping out of the car. "Mr. Cobb, we need to speak with you."

Bernie whipped his head around. "Detectives? What are you doing here?"

Charli pulled out her notebook and pen. "We needed to speak with you right away. I'm afraid it's urgent."

The funeral director's mouth opened and closed several times before he spoke. "What? Did you find out something about Candace?" He swallowed hard. "Or Jacob?"

Matthew cleared his throat. "Before we get into any specifics, we need to ask what you were doing last night."

Bernie's gaze darted between the detectives, and for a moment, Charli thought he might take flight. He didn't, though his mouth pressed into a tight line. "Last night? Uh, nothing, really. I got off work at eight. I had dinner. Went to sleep at ten, and was at work at eight this morning, as usual. Why?"

Charli studied his face carefully. "Can anyone confirm this?"

Bernie threw his hands in the air, his keys flying over his head and landing with a rattle. "No. I live alone. Can someone explain to me why what I was doing last night is relevant to your case?"

Knowing she might as well rip the bandage off, Charli took in a deep breath. "I'm sorry to be the one to tell you, but Jacob was found murdered this morning."

Cobb's hand jumped to cover his mouth, and he swayed on his feet. "Murdered? How? When?"

Charli took his arm, steadying him. "We can't discuss the details, but we're sorry for your loss."

Cobb's expression turned glacial. "Surely...surely you don't think..." He paled. "Is that why you were asking about last night? I'd never do that."

"Do what, exactly?" Charli needed to push him harder, needed more of a reaction.

The director's mouth dropped open. The light in his eyes dissipated, leaving empty hazel circles. "I-I don't understand. How could this happen? Two of my employees go missing and... Jacob is dead?"

It was the first time Charli had witnessed a softer side to Bernie. "That is what we wanted to talk to you about. Do you know of anyone who may have benefited from Mr. Pernell's death?"

"Of course not. Jacob was a kind man. He came to work, he did his job, and he went home to his wife and son. I can't see him doing anything to rattle anyone." The wrinkles that normally adorned Cobb's grumpy forehead had fallen slightly. His eyebrows were no longer raised in anger but curiosity.

"How would you describe your relationship with Mr. Pernell?" Matthew kept his tone light.

Bernie rubbed the fabric of his wrinkle-free tie between his finger and thumb. "We had a great relationship. He was a good employee."

Matthew fired the next question while Charli watched for any hint that Cobb was lying. "Could you tell us about the last conversation you had with him?"

Bernie blew out a long, shuddered breath. "Oh my god. I texted him last night. I was criticizing him. He was my best employee, and the last thing I did was reprimand him for deviating from procedure. I'm a monster."

Frankly, Cobb *had* seemed like a monstrous boss. He couldn't have been easy to work for, considering how he'd barked orders at other employees at the funeral home, but this existential realization appeared genuine. There was a deep regret pooling in the tears on his cheek.

"How did he deviate from procedure, exactly?" Though Cobb was clearly upset, Charli didn't have the luxury of ending her partner's line of questioning.

And continuing to question a suspect who appeared distraught was a tactic she'd used in the past. If someone was genuinely devastated, continuing to question them would only prolong their sadness. But when the emotion was faked, and it didn't garnish sympathy from the detectives, the suspect would grow angry that they weren't believed. They'd be crying one second and snapping the next with no provocation. It was an excellent method for weeding out false emotions.

Bernie ran a hand through his once-red hair. "It's nothing. Getting upset with Jacob seems so unimportant now. But we have a very detailed way we do our paperwork. On the last case we did, before he stopped showing up for work, there was a page out of order. Honestly, it didn't even matter to me much. I was just angry at that point, and I'd have found anything to nitpick him on."

"I can see how that might be frustrating, but do you always reprimand your employees with a text message?" Charli was doing her best to get righteous anger to form in Cobb's heart.

But no anger came, only more sorrow. His face contorted, lips turning downward while recounting his last words to Jacob. "It's stupid, really. Clearly, he had more going on in his life. I knew from a phone call with him that he was rattled. And yet I only wanted him to come to work. And to think, if he'd done what I wanted, more of my employees may have ended up shot."

Matthew rubbed the stitches on his arm through his shirt. "But why are your employees disappearing to begin with? Surely you have some inclination of what could be going on at the funeral home to cause this."

"There isn't a reason, to my knowledge. But nobody talks to me much about their personal lives. And I guess now we can see why." Cobb's gaze dropped to the ground.

Either Cobb had an amazing hold on his emotional reactions, or his regret was real.

After another twenty minutes of futile questioning, Matthew excused himself and Charli, and Cobb picked up his keys, wiping a tear from his eye.

Once the door was closed behind him, Charli shook her

head in frustration. "Man, you've got to be a real workaholic to have an existential crisis and then proceed to go to work."

Matthew raised his eyebrows. "Like we're ones to talk. Hey, sometimes your work gets you out of your head when you're depressed. Nobody knows that better than me. And I think you know it too."

Charli didn't answer. Her gaze was fixed on a midnight black Escalade in the distance. The windows were tinted all around, even the front windows, which were technically illegal. Still, through the tint, there was a faint figure, and Charli could swear the person was staring at them.

Mere seconds after Charli glimpsed the vehicle, it peeled off, driving right past the detectives at an unprecedented speed.

Matthew did a double take. "What the hell was that?"

"Someone was watching us." Charli studied the plates. "I don't know who the hell it was, but I think I spooked him... or her...or them." She just wasn't sure.

Matthew raised an eyebrow. "Watching us? Or watching Bernie Cobb?"

Charli jotted the number into her notebook and handed it to Matthew. "I'm not sure, but I've got his plate numbers. Call it in to Janice."

"There's that eagle-eye. I'm on it." A few minutes later, Matthew disconnected the call. "Marco DeStasio. Do you know him?"

Charli sorted through her mental rolodex. "Marco DeStasio. I don't recognize the name. Do you?" It certainly hadn't come up in their investigation.

Matthew stuffed his phone back in his coat pocket. "Nope. But I think we need to pay Marco a friendly visit."

"Me too, but not tonight." She examined the purple circles underneath her partner's eyes. "We both need some sleep."

If there was even a possibility that this man was the killer, Charli wasn't going to speak to him without being armed with information. Whoever he was, this murderer was intelligent. He knew what he was doing.

But so did Charli.

17

"Marco DeStasio has a spotless record. Not so much as a traffic ticket on this guy." Charli swiveled in her desk chair to turn to Matthew, who was downing his third cup of coffee of the morning. "You find anything?"

Matthew let out a long sigh. "The man has no social media to speak of. At least we've got an address."

Thirty minutes ago, Charli had been ready to speed over to this man's house and demand to know why he was outside of Cobb's place. But after discovering such little information, she had to wonder if she was making a bigger deal out of this vehicle than she should have been.

Charli ran her fingers through her short hair, pushing her bangs away from her eyes. "Maybe he wasn't watching Bernie at all. I mean, maybe the guy had an angry phone call he was on, or he sped away because he realized he was late for work. We really don't know." For all they knew, it may not have even been DeStasio in the car. He was the vehicle's owner, but perhaps another family member had been driving.

Matthew rubbed the five o'clock shadow that had formed

on his chin, as it often did when they had hectic caseloads. "Let's just keep him on our list. We don't need to rush over to him right away, but I'm not ready to write this off, either. Something weird happened here, and my gut is telling me to keep an eye on this guy."

Charli wasn't going to be rude, but it wouldn't be the first time Matthew's gut had said something and ended up being wrong. Hell, sometimes his gut told him that a drive-through taco joint was a good choice at midnight. His gut had questionable decision-making skills that Charli didn't always trust. She preferred to rely on good old-fashioned evidence.

"So, where do we go from here, then? We've already interviewed all the employees, most of which went nowhere. We've got an APB on Elwood Sanders and have requested a warrant to search Cobb's home and vehicle. Maybe I should just…"

Charli pulled up the video footage of the night Candace went missing. She'd watched it several times over but held out hope that there was something she'd missed.

Matthew leaned back in his chair and groaned. "Charli, you've got that security footage covered. Trust me. If we're going to find a break in the case, it won't be from there."

Ruth rapped her knuckles against the doorframe. "You need a break, huh? Well, here I am, the break fairy. And I'm happy to work my magic." The sergeant's tone was so dry, as usual, that even her joke sounded serious.

"What break is that?" Charli swiveled to face her.

"We've got the warrant for Cobb's car. From what I've heard of your descriptions of him, I'm sure he'll be pleased." Ruth was just filled with sarcasm this morning.

Charli and Matthew had not exactly been generous in their descriptions of Cobb, but in retrospect, Charli felt for the man. He truly had seemed distraught by the news of Jacob's passing, which was odd, considering how unconcerned he'd been about Candace's disappearance. But perhaps he had time to process that news, or maybe he still believed her to be alive. Regardless, perhaps Cobb wasn't the monster he'd initially appeared to be.

But that didn't mean Charli would not do everything she could to investigate the man, which meant searching his car. If that upset him, well, so be it. Charli hadn't become a detective to coddle anyone's feelings.

"We'll go over there now to let him know the forensics team is on their way and ensure he doesn't go back into the car to change anything." Charli was already rising from her chair.

"Good. Go get me the bad guys." Ruth disappeared into the hall as quickly as she'd come. She had a knack for that.

Charli wasn't so sure this warrant was going to bring the killer to justice, but it was worth a shot.

Getting ready to shut off her computer, Charli froze in her spot. Only her forefinger moved to press the space bar down.

Matthew hurried to look over her shoulder. "I know that look. That's your golden retriever look. You find something, Lassie?"

Charli held up a finger. "First of all, do you think Lassie was a golden retriever? But, yes, I think so. You know that car we've been seeing in the background?"

"Yeah. It barely blips in the corner. But there's not much we can do with that. We can't see enough to give us a make or model."

"Maybe not but look at that! Hold on, let me take it back a few seconds. It's so fast, but if I pause here..."

Matthew gasped. "Shit, you're right. That's a partial plate in the other car's reflection. I bet we can get Cyber to clean it up enough to make them out. Good eye, Charli."

With just a few numbers, they'd be able to run the partial

and ideally get a list of potential cars that ended with those digits.

Charli nodded her thanks, a slow grin spreading across her face. "I'll get this sent in now. Maybe by the time we're done with Cobb, we'll have more answers."

Charli had to think steps ahead. If Cobb was a dead end, she wanted another road to go down. This was her favorite part of her job, playing chess. Although she always aimed to be a few moves ahead of the criminal she was hunting down, that was easier said than done. In this case, their leads were sparse, and the leads they did have were only vaguely connected to the case.

After submitting the request to run the partial plate, Charli and Matthew made their way to Kirkland Funeral Home.

Upon pulling the door open, Charli nearly ran into Lee Kirkland.

His drooping, dull eyes took a moment to register the encounter. But once he processed Charli and Matthew's presence, deep grooves formed above his brow.

The owner checked his sleek gold watch. There was no doubt in Charli's mind the piece was expensive. "Shouldn't you two be busy finishing your investigation? I wanna know what the hell happened in my funeral home."

Charli straightened. "That's exactly what we're trying to do. Do you know where Bernie Cobb is?"

Without breaking eye contact, Lee bellowed out. "Bernie! Those detectives are back."

Not a moment later, the door to the back room swung open, and Bernie was moving toward the detectives. Whatever sadness Charli had witnessed from him earlier had dissipated. His face mirrored Lee's, but the grooves in his forehead weren't quite so deep yet.

"You had more questions about Jacob?" Bernie straightened his suit jacket, his foot tapping a rhythm against the tile floor.

"Actually, we've got our forensics team on-site, and I wanted to inform you we have a search warrant for your car." Charli pulled the warrant from her pocket and handed it to him.

Man, Charli had thought she'd seen Bernie angry before, but the rage that flowed out of him like an exploding volcano was fiery enough to burn the entire funeral home down. His face was as red as lava.

Bernie's fists balled up at his sides. "You want to search my car? Why the hell would you need to do that?"

"We're exhausting every avenue to find out what happened at this funeral home and to your employees. Surely you want to get to the bottom of this as much as we do." Matthew kept his voice soft and steady.

But that wasn't enough to keep either Bernie or Lee Kirkland relaxed.

Lee moved in front of Bernie, practically pushing him backward. "Are you accusing my funeral home manager of being involved in this? Bernie might be an imbecile, but he's no killer. What kind of cops are you?"

Bernie's face turned a brighter shade of red. "An imbecile? Are you kidding me? I keep this place going while you get drunk on wine coolers in the Bahamas."

The hunched-over man thrust a finger in Bernie's chest, forcing him to stagger a few steps back. "I earned my right to get drunk in the Bahamas! I've put in my time, and I've done a much better job than you ever have!"

The door behind Lee swung open, interrupting their conversation. A blond man with neatly trimmed facial hair waved down the director. "Sir, I just spoke to the Jacksons about today's service. They wanted to see if you'd received the slideshow they emailed you."

A flash of annoyance crossed Bernie's already red face. "I received the slideshow, but I've been a little busy, Richard."

Wait, did this man work for Cobb? They'd never interviewed him. Charli flashed the director a questioning look. "Who is this?"

The director waved a hand in the man's direction. "My assistant, Richard."

Matthew cocked his head. "How come he wasn't on the list of employees you gave us?"

Bernie plastered a patronizing smile on his face. "Because he was on paternity leave. The man hasn't even been here in several weeks. He's of no use to your investigation. I only called him in after Jacob failed to show up for work."

Mr. Kirkland threw his hands in the air. "Paternity leave? What the hell is that? Did you spit a baby out of your asshole?"

The color drained from the assistant's face. "No, sir, but my wife—"

"Gentlemen, please." Charli held up a hand. "We all have a lot going on but getting upset won't do anyone any good."

Without giving Mr. Kirkland another glance, she turned to the assistant. "What's your last name, Richard?" Although the man hadn't been to work in a while, he likely knew Candace and Jacob. He certainly could have had access to the building.

"Godfrey." The color had returned to the assistant's face.

Matthew cleared his throat. "Any other employees on temporary leave you'd like to tell us about, Mr. Cobb?"

"No. He's the only one." Bernie's jaw slid from side to side, his teeth clenched together. "Look, do your search. I'm not going to tell you how to do your job, even if you're clearly failing miserably. But I'm going to go do mine. Just stay out in the parking lot. I've got a funeral in a few hours, and that family does not deserve to see you as they mourn their loved one."

Fair enough. Charli had done her job by informing Cobb of the search. She had no interest in staying at the funeral home to make mourners uncomfortable.

Though she did plan to circle back to this Richard Godfrey. Obviously, now wasn't a great time, but they needed all the information they could get.

Cobb stormed off, Godfrey in tow, leaving Charli and Matthew with a glaring Lee Kirkland.

Charli didn't mind, as sour as the man was. She had a few questions for him.

"Sir, can you tell us of your whereabouts last night after five p.m.?" Charli kept her tone light, a gentle smile on her face. She hoped it would keep Lee's anger from rising, but evidently, that was too much to ask for.

"Oh, so now you're going to accuse me of murder too?" The loose jowl skin on his cheeks rose and fell with his exaggerated tone. "For your information, I spent the evening at Maestro's Restaurant with my infuriating crow of a wife. I took her to a boring play afterward. I've got one of those fancy new cars with GPS, so I can prove exactly where I was. You aren't pinning anything on me, coppers."

Charli ignored the outburst. "And what can you tell us about Jacob Pernell?"

"Who?" Lee raised his eyebrows. His face was so different when it wasn't scrunched up like a crumpled piece of paper.

Matthew tapped his foot. The motion wasn't overly aggressive, but Charli knew this to be a sign of Matthew's growing indignation with an interview subject. "You know, your employee who died."

Lee's softened expression disappeared as quickly as it had arrived. "Didn't know the fellow! Now, I think Bernie was clear with you. Go do your business in the parking lot so you can find out my funeral home manager and I had nothing to do with this."

"Of course, sir." Charli didn't have any more questions for him, anyway. The man was clueless about his own operation. They could follow up on those GPS coordinates later, as well as CCTV coverage and restaurant receipts.

Once outside, Charli and Matthew let the smiles they were repressing come to the surface.

"You know, Charli, something tells me that man is not a big fan of yours."

"I think you're right. Now come on, copper. Let's head to Bernie's vehicle and see what we can find."

Matthew chuckled. "Right behind you, Deputy Dan."

18

Charli popped a fry into her mouth, letting the salt melt against her tongue. It was one of her last fries, so she savored it before drowning it in a mouthful of chocolate milkshake.

Matthew sucked down the rest of his own strawberry shake. "What would we do without fast-food delivery services?"

She chuckled before slurping down the last bit of her icy drink. "Starve, I guess."

Charli and Matthew had decided together that the best thing for them to do was interview Richard Godfrey next. As Bernie Cobb's right-hand man, Richard could potentially hold some vital information about the day-to-day operations of the funeral home. And as they scarfed down their food in the parking lot at the funeral home, they took a few minutes to compare notes on the investigation.

Officer Langston, who was at his post in the parking lot, had promised to let the detectives know if their next interviewee left the building before they had a chance to find him inside.

Charli's car wasn't parked far from Cobb's, where the forensics team was finishing up their work. She and Matthew had been peeking in from time to time, though nothing overtly incriminating had been found. There were some prints and human hair found throughout the vehicle, but those could belong to anyone. They'd have to wait for lab results for anything conclusive.

Charli was stuffing the wrappers from her burger and fries into the paper fast-food bag when Matthew's head snapped up. "Officer Langston is waving us over. Let's get to Godfrey before he reaches his car."

Charli's boots were already hitting the pavement. They cut Richard off in front of the first row of parked cars.

Matthew strode toward the assistant. "Mr. Godfrey, could we speak to you for a moment?"

Godfrey's bright eyes looked Matthew up and down. He couldn't have been taller than five-seven, and Matthew towered over him. Charli would forever be jealous of how Matthew could intimidate people with his height alone.

"Uh, sure. What can I help you with?" Richard studied the detectives and pushed a pair of black-rimmed glasses up on his nose.

Charli clicked her pen and poised it over her notebook. "We'd love to talk to you about Candace Redding. When was the last time you saw her?"

Richard rubbed his bearded jaw. "I'm not sure. I mean, it was definitely over a month ago, but I can't remember our last encounter specifically. She worked with me on my last shift before my wife gave birth to our baby, so I know we spoke that day. But about what, I'm not sure."

Richard had high cheekbones, a square jaw, and rugged good looks. Charli could picture him on the front cover of a magazine. It was plausible that Candace could have found Richard attractive.

"How long have you known Ms. Redding?"

Richard shrugged. "I think I've been working for Cobb for about four years now. She was already an employee when I started."

Charli gave a slow nod. "What kind of relationship did you and Ms. Redding have?"

There wasn't even a flicker of emotion on his face when Godfrey spoke next. "We had a fine relationship, I think. We only spoke about work, not much else. But she was good at her job. Other employees had it out for her, but I like anyone who can work effectively, so she was okay, in my book."

Charli noted that Godfrey spoke about Candace in the past tense, though they weren't at all certain she was officially dead. Interesting.

Matthew shifted his weight to his right leg as he slid one hand into his pocket. "What didn't other employees like about her?"

Richard pushed his glasses up on his nose again. "Oh, you know. It was petty shit. The girls didn't like her because they thought she was too flirty. The men didn't like that they couldn't date her. Stuff that really shouldn't matter in a work environment. I mean, sure, the girl was a little flirty, but I never noticed her doing anything inappropriate."

The term was vague, so Charli needed to clarify. "What do you mean by 'inappropriate'?"

"Well, I don't think she had any affairs with anyone at work, if you know what I mean. But I try to avoid office gossip." Richard craned his neck to peer around the detectives toward his car. "Look, is this going to take much longer? I have a limited amount of time for lunch."

"It won't take much longer. We really appreciate your cooperation." Charli had to keep Godfrey talking. "What kind of things did you and Ms. Redding talk about?"

Richard rolled his shoulders while letting out a long sigh.

"We seriously only talked about work. If she had a message from Cobb, she told me. We didn't get into anything else. I don't keep personal relationships with my coworkers."

"So, you didn't have a personal relationship with Jacob Pernell, either?" Matthew's head tilted to the right ever so slightly.

"No." Godfrey didn't even bother any further explanation. He stuffed his hands into his pockets and sighed.

Charli was determined to keep him talking, though. "And when was the last time you saw Jacob Pernell?"

"The same, about a month ago, prior to my paternity leave. If you're going to ask me about his personal life too, I really don't know anything. The guy kept to himself. And I come to work to do my job. I don't think I'm going to be of much help to you."

Charli couldn't decide if he was in a hurry to leave the conversation because he was hungry or because he had something to hide. "Can you tell us about Ms. Redding and Mr. Pernell's interactions with one another? Were they friends?"

Richard rubbed his forehead and let out a long sigh. "Maybe, but I really have no clue. Their conversations seemed normal to me. If you need to ask me more questions, can we do that later? I've already called in my food, and I don't want it to get cold."

Godfrey didn't wait for an answer. He was already moving in between Charli and Matthew, pushing through them slightly to get to a black SUV.

Charli's breath caught in her chest. "Is this your vehicle?"

"Yeah, why?" Godfrey's tone was growing sharper. Charli had been careful to make sure her words were not accusatory, but Godfrey didn't seem convinced.

Though Charli's heart had increased speed, she couldn't let Godfrey know that, so she shrugged. "And you said you haven't been to the funeral home at all since your paternity leave?"

"Not even once." He raised a single finger in emphasis. "So, whatever has happened here, I don't know anything about it. I wasn't even supposed to be back for a few more weeks, but Cobb said he really needed me at work after hearing about Jacob, so I did him a favor. Now, if you'll excuse me, Detectives."

Charli smiled as she tucked her notebook away and reached for her phone from inside her jacket. "Thank you for your cooperation."

As Richard Godfrey's door slammed, Charli surreptitiously took a snapshot of his license plate before moving out of the way so he could back out of his space. It was a swift enough move that Godfrey likely didn't notice, but Matthew sure did.

"What was that about?"

Charli had to bite her lip to contain the excitement building up within her. "He's lying about never being at the funeral home during his paternity leave. And I think I can prove it."

19

Charli was rarely tempted to speed, but it took all her effort to follow the traffic laws on the way back to the precinct. Prior to now, there was no concrete evidence regarding who was at the funeral home the night Candace disappeared.

She glanced at her partner, careful not to take her eyes off the road for long. "Godfrey's car definitely looks like the one in the security footage. If we can get the partial plate to match, we'll know he's lying."

Sure, Charli had noticed the partial plate before they went back to the funeral home, but partial plates meant sifting through a pile of potential vehicle owners. Now, Charli was pretty sure they'd found exactly who owned the car.

"If you're right about this, Charli, it'll be a major break in the case." Matthew echoed her thoughts as Charli pulled into a parking space outside the precinct. He unbuckled his seat belt, leaning over to fumble with the door handle with his left hand.

"Godfrey's car definitely looks like the one in the security footage. If we can get a match on the plates, then he could be involved in whatever happened that night, or at least know something about it."

There was no other legitimate reason for Godfrey to be driving outside of the funeral home in the wee hours of the morning when he had a newborn baby back at home who needed his attention. Of course, it was possible someone else was driving Godfrey's car, but even if that was the case, Godfrey would likely know who had access to his vehicle. Finally, they were homing in on what happened that night.

Matthew pulled the front door open for Charli with his good arm, an act of chivalry she'd normally refuse. But she was way too eager to get back to their office to argue about him getting the door for her. "Thank you."

The air-conditioned breeze blew Matthew's hair back, making his receding hairline that much more pronounced. "As soon as we can determine whether the plates match, we need to bring him back in for questioning and—"

"Detective Cross?" Another voice pulled Charli away from what Matthew was saying.

Charli hadn't even made it to her office when a young blonde intern with pink lip gloss grabbed her attention. "Yes?"

"So sorry to interrupt." Her gaze shifted between Matthew and Charli before moving down to the floor. "But I have mail for you."

"For me?" Charli rarely got mail at the precinct.

The intern placed a flat white envelope in Charli's hand before scurrying away. Charli squinted down at it.

"There's no return address." Matthew peeked over her shoulder. "You should be careful with that."

"It's a letter-sized envelope, Matt. What's it going to be? The world's smallest bomb? Besides, it's postmarked. It's not like it was hand-delivered." Charli would be more concerned if it was. It wasn't uncommon for a criminal to hand-deliver a package to avoid being caught by the postal service.

"I mean, you can do dangerous things with small envelopes. What about anthrax?"

Charli let out a croak of a laugh. "You did not just say anthrax. What year are we in?"

"I'm just saying, stuff happens." Matthew continued his stride down the hall, and Charli followed.

"I don't think I'm important enough for anyone to go through the trouble of sending me anthrax." Anthrax was difficult to attain. "It's probably a letter from a victim's family or something."

It wouldn't be the first time Charli had been thanked, but she usually got phone calls instead of letters. Still, Charli couldn't shake the thought that the letter could be something more sinister. She might as well throw some gloves on, just in case.

They were just inside their office door when Charli tore the seal on the envelope and pulled out the printer paper inside. She studied the small black font before beginning to read it. For a thank-you letter, it was surprisingly short. In fact, there was just one line.

But that one line changed everything.

The world moved in slow motion, as though it was falling off its axis. The words blurred together, and Charli had to read one more time to make sure she wasn't imagining things. But repeating the words in her mind only caused the room to spin faster. Her legs were frozen in place, but still, she thought she might fall over.

"Charli, you okay? What is it?" Matthew slid on his own gloves before reaching for the letter, and because Charli couldn't explain anything at the moment, she let him slide it from her fingertips.

Matthew read the letter aloud, confirming what Charli

had read was real. "Ten years and you still haven't found me. Do you give up?"

Charli was a statue. Her partner's words were a distant echo, as though she were hearing them underwater. If she shut her eyes, she felt underwater too, like when she and Madeline used to drift in the community pool when they were just little girls.

What Charli wouldn't give to be floating with her now.

"What is this, Charli?"

Charli was asking herself the same question. She didn't want to believe it...but, no, it could only mean one thing. The ten years made the sentiment abundantly clear.

"It's from Madeline's killer."

"What?" Matthew gasped, but Charli didn't catch his expression. She couldn't look at him. She couldn't look at anything. "How can you be sure?"

Charli could explain it, and she would, but not yet. She could barely catch her breath.

"I need water." The words came out of her mouth without conscious effort. *Why had she asked for water?* She wasn't thirsty.

Matthew put a hand on his partner's arm. "Come on, Charli. I'll get you a bottle. Sit down, and I'll be right back."

He led Charli to her chair, but once she was sitting, she hardly remembered getting there. Minutes dragged by before the world came back to focus. By the time she'd processed what she'd read, Matthew still hadn't returned.

Charli had learned years ago that it was better when the world was fading from her. Because once she felt her feet firmly planted on the ground again, the emotions came crashing toward her like a train barreling down the tracks, threatening to derail her from the job she had to attend to.

And if this train derailed her, it would be a first. Charli had always relied on her work to save her from negative feelings. But this...brief but brutal message consumed her more than anything had since she'd lost Madeline nearly a decade ago.

Could it really be him? The man who had stolen Madeline from her? Who had mutilated her body beyond recognition?

But why? Why send Charli a letter after all these years? There hadn't been even a trace of the man in the past decade. If there had, she would've been hot on his trail. A part of Charli had considered that perhaps the man had died. There weren't any other kidnappings and murders after Madeline. Statistically, men like that usually weren't satisfied with taking just one woman. Surely the killer had either moved away or died. And she hoped every day for the latter.

But he wasn't dead.

This letter ripped those hopes into shreds. The killer was alive and well, watching her. Unless this was some kind of sick joke, this person knew where Charli was, where she worked, and she didn't know a thing about him.

Faster than a flip of a dime, horror slid into rage. A red-hot fire consumed Charli so entirely she could feel the heat on her palms.

That bastard.

The sensation of floating in water returned to Charli once more. This time, she was in a pool of her own rage with the waves of that rage trying to drown her.

"Come on, Charli. You have to arch your back further than that!" Madeline was standing in the shallow end of the pool, her hands underneath Charli.

But Charli continued to feel herself sinking. She could only float for a few seconds before the waves of the pool rolled over her stomach, dragging her down into the depths. Although this depth was only three feet, the sensation of sinking wasn't pleasant.

Charli rolled onto her feet, planting them firmly in front of

Madeline's. "I just can't do it. I can't float like you. I have no idea how you keep your body on top of the water like that."

They'd been swimming together since they were little girls, but Charli had never had formal lessons. She'd learned to swim right here, in the community pool of Madeline's grandmother's apartment. They'd spend most of the summer at this pool, when the sweltering Savannah heat kept them from all other activities.

"Oh my gosh, Charli. The problem is you just don't know how to relax. You have to let your body become one with the water. I always take one deep breath in, and then I float away."

Madeline was good at that. She always had been. But already, at age thirteen, Charli had the weight of the world on her shoulders. Her grandma's health was declining, which caused a lot of stress in her home. At the same time, she was trying to keep her straight-A average.

"What does that even mean? I can't become one with the water! I'm a human, and it's not!"

Madeline folded her wet arms together on top of her hot pink one-piece swimsuit. "Humans are sixty percent water, you know." Madeline loved statistics just as much as Charli did.

Charli's hands flew into the air, spraying Madeline with excess water. "Fine! If you want me to drink the pool, then I can become one with it. But without doing that, this is basically nonsense!"

Madeline chuckled to herself, though Charli was quite serious. Madeline never took her best friend's freak-outs seriously.

"Charli, I don't know why you've always got to try so hard. We aren't even in high school yet, but you're studying like your life depends on it. You don't even know where you're going to go to college! You don't know what you want to be when you grow up. Just have some fun!"

Madeline was so good at that, living in the moment. She celebrated every day like it was her last. There was something kind of cosmic about it all. Madeline had said multiple times she had no interest in planning for the future. Was it because she would never get one?

A nearby kid, some blonde six-year-old in floaties, hit a beach ball square at Charli's head. It bounced off into the concrete, and even she couldn't help but laugh. The blue, green, and yellow ball provided a nice break from Charli's stress.

And Madeline was right. Why was learning to float such a stress-filled event? It was impossible for Charli to come across a task she didn't take seriously. With everything she did, she put her all into it. Floating didn't require effort, but the lack thereof. It required Charli to allow her worries to float away along with her body.

Madeline put her hand on Charli's back. "Okay, this time, I'm going to completely hold you up. I'm never going to let go, so you don't have to try to float. Just lay on top of my hands."

Charli shook her head slightly, sending her wet raven hair flying. "But that isn't going to help me learn. What's the point?"

Now it was Madeline's turn to groan. "Charli, you just have to trust me. Do you trust me?"

She did. More than anyone in the world, more than even her parents, Charli trusted her best friend. Madeline knew everything about her. She was the only one Charli shared her innermost thoughts with. Still, she didn't believe this was going to help her float. But she'd suppress the doubt to please her best friend.

Charli leaned back once more, feeling two palms on her upper and lower back. The situation felt a little silly, as she imagined all the soccer moms tanning by the pool, watching Charli being held up in the water.

"Now, close your eyes. This is what floating feels like."

Charli followed Madeline's instructions, but she couldn't control her defiance. "It's not, though. It's not what floating feels like. If I was floating, I wouldn't feel your hands on my back. I mean, I'm not even doing anything. My body is totally limp."

"Exactly! You're supposed to be limp!"

This was a foreign concept for Charli. How could she go limp without the security of Madeline holding her up? It was one thing to float there motionless, knowing that Madeline wouldn't let her fall. But if she relaxed her body normally, she'd sink to the bottom of the pool like a backpack full of rocks.

"Madeline, I'm never going to be able to do this without you holding me up. Let's just go do something else. You said your mom packed us a lunch, right? I'm getting hungry."

"Yeah, yeah. We'll eat in a second. But just so you know, you're doing it."

Charli's eyes snapped open. "What?"

"Look, Charli! I'm not holding on!"

Sure enough, when Charli looked down at her body, Madeline was a good foot or two away, holding up her hands.

"Oh my gosh! I'm really doing it!" Charli let out a honk of a laugh. Of course, the moment she did, the air escaping her lungs caused her to sink into the pool.

But it didn't matter. She had done it. Charli had floated. And since she'd briefly felt the sensation, she had been able to repeat it again and again.

"See, didn't I tell you? You just needed to relax."

Madeline was the only one who could teach Charli how to do that. How it came so naturally to her friend, Charli would never know. Sometimes, she envied Madeline's free spirit. But most of the time, she was just grateful that she had a best friend who could help her with the aspects of life that were so hard for her.

Charli and Madeline spent the rest of the afternoon floating and eating the lunch her mom had packed. BLTs and salted potato chips. The salt hung on the tip of Charli's tongue, and she savored every bite. Why did potato chips taste so much better after a long swim?

"Charli?"

Charli didn't know how long Matthew and Ruth had been standing in the door. She'd been staring at her computer monitor in front of her but not seeing it, not really. The only images she could see now were flashbacks to Madeline's face.

She shifted her face toward them but said nothing, not a muscle on her face flinching.

Ruth studied her, a gaze so intense Charli had only witnessed her use while speaking with a victim's family. And Charli didn't like it. She would not go back to that, being just a loved one of a victim. She was a detective now, and there was a power she held now that high-school Charli could only have dreamed of.

Charli took a slow breath, and then another. She hadn't even realized she'd been holding her breath. "You guys can stop looking at me like that. I'm okay."

Matthew walked over and handed her an icy water bottle. Charli didn't drink it, though, just palmed it in hopes that the cool water would soothe the lava of fury pulsing through her veins.

"Maybe you should go home for the day, Detective Cross." Ruth wasn't barking an order, as she usually did. She simply offered Charli the option.

But the option wasn't viable to Charli. She straightened her back, pulling her shoulders taut. "I need to be here. You need me here."

Ruth kept her gaze on Charli's. "What I need is a functioning detective. I'm not so sure you're in a position to act as that right now."

As Ruth stepped forward, Matthew wilted back. Charli could interpret her partner's silence. Matthew would've jumped to Charli's defense if he thought she should stay at work. Both of them wanted her to go home.

"I am a functioning detective. Watch." Charli turned to Matthew. "Did you bag that letter?"

Matthew cleared his throat. "Yes, of course."

"Good. We need to run it for prints." Charli had little hope that this would result in anything helpful. Numerous people had touched that envelope, and there would be prints all over it. Perhaps they'd be able to find DNA on the glue. "And that intern. Let's find her and see where she got that letter."

Matthew bit the corner of his lip, as though he knew what he was about to say would disappoint Charli. "I already did. It was just in the mailbox, Charli. Run of the mill postage. All we have is an approximate location of where it was sent from, Greensboro. Sent about four days ago."

So, he was living in North Carolina? No, Charli had to stop her mind from jumping to conclusions. It was easy to want to do so. This was Madeline she was seeking justice for, after all. But she couldn't let her emotions cloud her judgment.

Ruth was likely right. Charli wasn't going to do her best work right now, but she couldn't admit to that. Appearing rock solid to everyone around her was vital. If she seemed okay, perhaps Ruth would agree to her next request.

"I want back on the case." Charli tossed her shoulders back.

Ruth's chest rose and fell with a long breath. Her gaze shifted between Matthew and Charli. "Are you sure this isn't just someone messing with you?"

"I'm positive." Actually, she wasn't. Charli had no way of knowing who sent the letter. It wasn't like the envelope or note had any specific details.

Anyone who knew Charli personally was aware of her relationship with Madeline. Determining that the ten-year anniversary was about to arise would be easy to do. Hell, the suspect in her last case had figured out Charli's connection to Madeline by reading an old yearbook at the local library.

It was possible someone other than Madeline's killer had sent this.

But why would they? What would be the point? And Charli couldn't agree with Ruth that it might be a prank on her. If she did, Ruth would never allow her to reopen the case.

"Cross, you worked on that case for ages and only came up with dead ends. You're a skilled detective. If there was a trail to follow, you would have been on it already. I know this must stir up a lot of emotions for you, but opening Madeline's case back up is not the answer."

"But I just think—"

Ruth held up a finger. "Right now, I need you to focus on the case at hand, unless you need to take some time off." Ruth folded her arms, a move she rarely made. The sergeant wouldn't budge on her stance.

Charli leaned back in her chair, shoulders deflated. "No, I don't need time off."

Ruth uncrossed her arms, letting them fall at her sides. Relief shone in her brown eyes. "Good. Because forensics has called to say the hair they found in the back of Cobb's car was red and the approximate length of Candace's based on recent photos. It'll take some time to get a concrete identification, but it's enough of a lead that you can return to Cobb and pry about this hair."

Right. Red hair was uncommon enough that if it was found in the back of Cobb's car, he should be able to identify who it belonged to. Was it a friend? A family member? The funeral director was a redhead himself, after all. And so was his assistant. Or did it belong to Candace, and if so, what was she doing in the back of his vehicle?

How many redheads did the funeral home have, anyway?

Normally, Charli would be running through all the possible scenarios in her mind, but at the moment, her brain was as frozen as a mountain lake in January. She couldn't get herself to refocus on the task at hand, but maybe the car ride over would help.

"We can go back over there right away." Charli stood from her chair.

Matthew, who until now had been leaned against the window, stepped forward. Charli hadn't been paying him the slightest attention. Her focus was on Ruth. Now that she'd gotten a glimpse of her partner, she saw the strained smile on his face. He was worried about her.

But he grabbed his jacket off his desk, anyway. "Sure, let's head out."

Suddenly, Charli wasn't looking forward to the car ride. It was going to be filled with questions from Matthew about that letter.

And she wasn't sure she was ready to talk about it.

20

Five minutes of the drive had passed in complete silence. Although Charli initially preferred this to her partner's prying about her emotional state, the quiet offered little relief. She could sense Matthew's eyes boring into her, trying to read her every micro-expression.

Charli drummed her fingers against the steering wheel. "Just say what you wanna say. I can tell you're itching to ask."

Matthew pulled his phone from his pocket under his seat belt, pretending to look at it. "There's nothing I need to ask."

"Oh, really?" Charli's pixie-cut bangs shifted into her eyes when she bobbed her head toward Matthew. As if her sarcastic tone wasn't enough, she wanted to convey it with the look on her face.

Matthew ran his fingers across his receding hairline. "I'm just wondering if you're all right, Charli. Getting that letter was pretty crazy, and I can see it's affected you."

Charli hated that it did. She didn't hate missing Madeline or caring about her. She'd always love that girl to pieces. But it was abhorrent that the man who stole her life could have this much of an impact on Charli's emotional well-being. Hadn't that asshole taken enough from her?

"Why now?" Charli finally uttered the question that had been bouncing around her head like a rogue ping pong ball. "It's been a decade. I've never heard anything from him before, so why would he taunt me now?"

Charli couldn't look at Matthew. She was coming up on a turn and had to focus on incoming traffic. But the squeak of his body against the leather seat told her he was shifting uncomfortably.

"Do you think it's possible that he's not taunting you at all? Maybe Ruth is right, and this is someone else. I mean, like you said, why now?"

The freeze on Charli's brain was slowly melting, which meant she could analyze the situation a little more objectively. "Maybe he's been worried about being caught. He didn't want to give me any more clues, but now that the case has gone cold, he thinks he can get away with it. Maybe he likes to know he can stress me out on such a huge anniversary. It'll be ten years that Madeline has been gone."

That wasn't out of the realm of possibility. Charli had read many cases of serial killers who thrived on attention from their cases. When the interest fizzled out, the killer would send a letter to the police to get back on their radar.

Matthew pulled his shirt collar away from his neck. "So, you really don't think there's any way that this is just a random person trying to get to you?"

Charli could lie to Ruth but not to Matthew. "I know that's possible, but I need Ruth to treat this like it's the real thing. I need to be back on that case."

She could assume the letter was a fake and let it go, but what if it wasn't? What if the letter was really from the killer and Charli ignored it? Just the thought sent a wave of nausea through her body. To think of having a clue to her friend's killer and not following up? That was an insult to the justice Madeline deserved.

Charli used one hand to turn the wheel to the left. "If it is a fake, then there is no harm done. It's a waste of time, sure, but I've got time to waste for Madeline. But if it's real..."

Matthew raised one side of his mouth in a half-smile. "I get it, Charli. And I'll always be on your side on this. You know that. But I don't want you getting your hopes up. Be open to the possibility that this isn't really from Madeline's killer, so the drive to find him doesn't eat you alive."

Charli drew in a deep breath before glancing at her partner. "I'm not going to get my hopes up. Don't worry."

She couldn't do that. Even if the letter wasn't a fake, the chances of it leading to any substantial break in the case were thin. And Ruth was right. Charli was a fantastic and driven detective who had gone over the case with a fine-tooth comb and found nothing.

It wasn't hope that kept Charli going, but a sense of obligation. She had to do right by Madeline. Her friend was the reason she had become a detective in the first place.

The funeral home came into view, and Charli let out a long sigh of relief. It wasn't that she didn't trust Matthew enough to open up to him about Madeline. She did, and she had many times over. Charli just wasn't ready to talk to anyone about the situation right now.

Hell, she wasn't even ready to talk about it with herself. And going back into the funeral home to ask Cobb about the hairs in his car would turn off the incessant chatter in her brain. She hoped.

Charli wanted to reopen Madeline's case officially. She wasn't about to stop pestering Ruth about it, but the sergeant was going to be more apt to let her take that case if she figured out this one.

The funeral home parking lot was nearly empty. The

service Cobb had referred to must be over by now. Richard Godfrey's blond head popped out of the front door, and he zipped to his vehicle. Damn, Charli had been so shaken by the letter that she completely forgot to check Richard's plates before they left the precinct. That was definitely next on her list after speaking to Cobb.

The director followed Godfrey out, and Charli had to quicken her steps to catch up with him.

Cobb's head snapped up at the sound of Charli's feet against the concrete. Bernie rolled his eyes. "What now?"

Charli sucked in a deep breath once she reached Cobb. It probably wouldn't hurt for her to get back into her running routine. She'd been so busy with her cases lately that she hadn't had the time. "We wanted to follow up on the search of your vehicle."

"The search of my vehicle where you found nothing, I presume." Cobb stood straight, clearly confident that they had found nothing of value.

Which wasn't the case, but Charli couldn't reveal that yet. She would question Cobb before he knew they'd found something suspicious, so he'd be less on edge. And less eager for an attorney.

Matthew sauntered to Charli's side. "When was the last time you had another person in your vehicle?"

Cobb furrowed his brow. "I have no idea. Probably never. Nobody drives the car but me, if that's what you're asking."

Charli kept her tone light. "You may be the only one to drive it, but do you ever give anyone a ride? Maybe you carpooled with some of the funeral home employees?"

Cobb tapped his foot against the concrete sidewalk. "I don't think it would be appropriate for me to give my employees a ride to work. They work for me, and that feels too personal. So no, I have not."

Matthew put one hand up. "Just to be extremely clear,

you don't know of any time when another individual was in your vehicle?"

"Not any time in the past year, at least. I don't get out much. I run my business. Before that, I took a few dates out in my car, but it's been so long, I don't remember any details." Cobb narrowed his eyes. "Hell, I don't even recall their names."

That was what Charli needed to verify, and Cobb hadn't minced words. "If what you say is true, then can you please explain why the forensics team found a long red hair in your vehicle?"

Cobb's gaze shifted between the detectives. "I work with many bodies each and every day. Of course, you are going to find other hair in my car. It gets on my clothes. Believe it or not, dead bodies shed a lot of hair when you comb them."

That wouldn't be a horrible excuse, if it weren't for the location of the hair. "It was found in the back seat."

The director squeezed his eyes shut for a moment. He rubbed the back of his neck, his eyes popping open. "I mean, I might have thrown my jacket back there. Or maybe I was putting groceries in the back of my car. I'm sure there is a simple explanation for this."

Whether Cobb was tensing up because he had something to hide or simply because he hadn't expected hair to be found, Charli couldn't tell. But it couldn't hurt to continue to apply some pressure.

Charli had her notebook and pen ready. "And have any of the bodies you've worked on lately had red hair?"

Cobb's face contorted, the deep grooves in his face becoming more pronounced. Dark malice radiated from every pore. "Wait a second. I see what you're doing here. You're trying to say the hair belonged to Candace."

Matthew put two hands up. "Whoa, there. No need for

the anger. It's not an accusation. We simply need to know if you had any bodies you worked on recently with red hair."

Cobb tossed his arms into the air. "I don't know. I work on a lot of people. It's possible. What is not possible is Candace's hair being in my car. When will you people leave me alone? Don't you think it's hard enough to run a funeral home without all this constant chaos? I don't need this harassment."

Charli doubted they could get Cobb to calm down, but perhaps the parking lot wasn't the best place for this conversation. "Perhaps we can move into your office to discuss this."

"The only thing we need to discuss is how you're going to leave me alone. Stop harassing me or I will lawyer up and sue your department. The Kirklands are furious that cops keep showing up at the funeral home. You are going to cost me my job! Just stop it now!"

Cobb didn't wait for an answer. He pushed through Charli and Matthew, bumping Charli's shoulder in the process.

"Hey!" Fire blazed in Matthew's eyes. "You are getting dangerously close to assaulting an officer!"

Charli rested a hand on Matthew's arm. "Let it go, Matt. We don't need to escalate this. Like I told him, if it's Candace's hair, we're going to find out. It's a matter of time."

Matthew's eyes widened at her. "Are you all right?"

Since Charli had seen the letter, this was the first time she felt like laughing. "Matt, are you kidding? He barely tapped me. I think I'm gonna survive. Don't worry."

Matthew's wide eyes eased, but he still stared on at her intently. "Are you sure you're okay? I mean, truly okay?"

A trail of warmth trickled down Charli's spine. Matthew was the only person in the world these days to check in on her like this, and a small part of her wanted to wrap his arms around her as she sobbed over how badly she missed Madeline.

At the core of all her shock, anger, and fear, that was the underlying emotion. She missed her so terribly, and not even ten years had managed to soothe her grief. She was confident now that she'd be missing her forever.

Charli couldn't fall to pieces, though. She had to focus on the case at hand. If there was any hope of getting Ruth on her side, her composure had to stick around. And as well-intentioned as Matthew was, she just knew he would share her breakdown with Ruth, and it would wreck her chances of ever reopening the case.

But she needed a moment to fall apart, ideally with a glass of wine. At first, she wasn't sure who she could do that with since Matthew wasn't an option. But when she pulled out her phone and scrolled through her contacts, she realized exactly who would have a drink with her tonight. Charli typed out a text.

Have any plans tonight?

21

Charli had clearly underestimated just how traumatic getting that letter was. Now that she was back in her office chair, the previous wave of nausea came over her. She could so vividly feel that paper in between her fingers again.

"Charli? Everything all right?" Matthew's words pulled her back to herself.

It was getting hard to conceal just how shaken she was. "I'm fine. Just waiting for this to load. Oh, and here it is. So, this is from the night Candace went missing and—"

"No, it's not." Matthew pointed to the edge of the video. "Look, it's from the night before."

"What?" Charli peered at the screen. "Oh, dammit! That's not what the file said. Someone must have mislabeled it."

The disappointment rang out in Charli's mind like a chiming bell. This wasn't what she'd been hoping for. She wanted to prove that Godfrey's car was at the funeral home the night Candace disappeared, forcing a huge break in their case, but Godfrey being there the night before would not be the break she needed.

And if she didn't have the break she needed, she was that much further from reopening Madeline's case. Charli had already made the decision that she wouldn't ask Ruth about the case again until this one was solved. She didn't want to appear obsessed. It would only make her sergeant less apt to allow her to investigate.

Matthew patted Charli's shoulder. "Hey, don't stress. This is still valuable information. Richard told us he hadn't been to the funeral home even once since he left for paternity leave. This will confirm he lied, and if he lied about that, he could've been lying about something else."

Charli blew out a breath. "Right."

And, hell, maybe him being there the night before still signaled some involvement. Perhaps the funeral home needed to be prepped for the subsequent murders that would take place there. After all, the black SUV was still at the funeral home in the middle of the night. If Godfrey wasn't working, he had no reason to be there at such an odd hour.

Charli paused the video footage right as the SUV pulled up. She then slid her phone out of her pocket to check, and as expected, the license plate was a perfect match.

"That's him. That's his car." Charli smacked the table. "At least we could catch him in this lie."

"You want to head over to Godfrey's place now?" Matthew, who had been bending over Charli's shoulder, stood up straight once more. Charli often forgot about just how tall Matthew was until she had to look up at him while sitting down.

"Let's do it." Charli had no interest in waiting. She wanted to fly through this case as fast as humanly possible.

Like Candace and Jacob's homes, Richard Godfrey's house was unexpectedly gaudy. Godfrey's house was actually the most bougie home they'd been to so far. There was a private gate at the end of the drive with the letter "G" imprinted on the front. The gate was open, but it led up to an extremely long concrete drive decorated with diamond-shaped concrete tiles. In between each row of diamonds was perfectly mowed crisscrossed grass.

The image brought the financial aspect of this case back to the forefront of Charli's mind. "So, this man is the funeral director's assistant, but he has a nicer house than the funeral director himself? Where the hell are these people getting all their money?"

Matthew shrugged, grimacing when he moved his right arm a little too much. "I don't know. But I hope we're about to find out. That's Godfrey on the porch, right?"

Charli parked next to the white Victorian mansion. The white wraparound porch glistened in the sunlight. From the car window, Charli could see both Richard and his wife were perched on a patio swing, the sleeping baby cradled in his wife's arms. Charli assumed he was a little boy, based on the blue onesie dotted with elephants.

Each one of them shared the same shade of honey-blonde hair. If Charli didn't know any better, she'd assume Godfrey's wife was a relative instead of a spouse. But he had been on paternity leave, and there was the child.

Charli raised her hand to get Godfrey's attention as she exited the vehicle. From the driveway, the porch was only ten feet away. "Have we caught you at a bad time?"

His wife flipped her wavy blonde hair before shooting her husband a quizzical look. "Who is that?"

Richard fidgeted with the edge of the swinging bench, his fingers wrapping around the light wooden seat. "I thought we had already talked about everything you needed to know."

Matthew stretched his arms out as he got out of the

passenger side door. "Actually, it seems like you didn't tell us quite everything."

Richard's wife gently tapped her foot on the wooden floor, stopping the swing from moving. The sudden change in motion caused the baby to fuss, and she began to rock the infant back and forth. "Richard, who are these people?"

"Babe, you know how I told you about Candace and Jacob? These are the detectives investigating the case. They had some questions for me earlier." Richard shifted back toward the detectives. "Meet my wife, Alexandria Lauradale."

Why did that name sound so familiar? Charli was racking her brain when Matthew reminded her.

"As in Lauradale Engineering?"

Right, of course. It was an engineering firm at the edge of the city.

Alexandria continued to sway back and forth on the swing, the baby once again sound asleep. "That's right. My daddy's business. How can we help you, Detectives?"

The bags under Alexandria's eyes suggested she was sleep deprived, and not in the mood for company. The way she kept eyeing her husband, it seemed this conversation might go more smoothly without her listening in.

Charli smiled at the sleeping baby. "We would like to speak with your husband privately. Mr. Godfrey, would that be all right with you?"

Alexandria nudged her husband before studying the detectives. "Excuse me, but the baby is finally asleep, and I don't want to wake him. Whatever you need to ask Richard, you can do so in front of me." Charli didn't want to force them to separate because trying to do so would only cause more resistance.

Richard nodded at his wife and patted her hand. "Yes, you can speak to me with my wife present, Detectives. By the way, do you have any news about Candace?"

"We're working on some leads regarding Ms. Redding. Actually, Mr. Godfrey, we found a discrepancy in your statement." Matthew stepped onto the ivory porch, and Charli quickly followed, moving in front of the white craftsman-style door. Above the door, a beautiful stained-glass window reflected hues of purple and blue onto the white porch wood.

"A discrepancy?" Alexandria pinned her husband with her gaze.

Richard's entire body stiffened, his eyes going wide. Perspiration dotted his upper lip, and he broke his frozen posture to swipe it away on his sleeve. "Uh, what discrepancy are you talking about?"

"You said that you haven't been at the funeral home since the start of your paternity leave." Charli pulled her phone out of her pocket and flashed it toward Richard. "But as you can see, your vehicle appeared outside of the funeral home the night before Candace's disappearance."

Alexandria snapped to her feet, the baby still in her arms. "Are you kidding me, Richard? You said you were running errands! But you were back at that damn funeral home? You don't even need that stupid job, and you were running off to it during your paternity leave? What was that about?"

Charli was tempted to give the wife a high five. Lying men needed to be kicked in the balls.

Of course, it wasn't like they'd just shown her a video of Richard murdering Candace with his own two hands. It seemed an oddly dramatic reaction to such a small piece of information. But Charli sure wasn't going to stop their bickering. Perhaps they would spill some vital information.

"Alexandria, please, not now. It was nothing. I'll explain everything to you." Richard responded through gritted teeth. It only made his square jawline more pronounced.

The newborn let out a piercing cry, and his mother paced the porch in an effort to soothe him. "That explanation will have to wait." She gave her husband one last hard stare before turning to Charli and Matthew. "Please excuse me, Detectives. I've got a fussy baby on my hands." With that, Alexandria disappeared inside the house.

Matthew flashed Richard a smile. "It must be tough having a newborn. I remember when my daughter was that age. Are you guys getting any sleep?"

Richard rubbed a hand through his hair. "Tell me about it. I feel like I could sleep for a week." He glanced over his shoulder at the door and lowered his voice. "Officers, would you mind following me to the end of the drive so we can speak in private?"

"Sure." Charli backed up to make room for Richard to leave the porch.

Once at the end of the drive, Godfrey wasted no time in admitting the truth. "Okay, I was at the funeral home, but I didn't tell you because I didn't want anyone to know why I was there. And nobody can know, not Cobb, not my wife, nobody. Hell, especially not my wife."

With their suspect showing an interest in being honest, Charli planned to ride that wave as long as humanly possible, which meant empathizing with Richard's position. "Your wife seems pretty stressed out."

Godfrey raised both eyebrows, making his blue eyes brighten. "Yeah, no joke. But it's nothing new. She's always stressed out."

If her parents were millionaires, that explained the beautiful house. "When she said you didn't have to work at the funeral home, was that her implying you didn't need to work at all because of her family's money?"

"Yes. She's been hinting for a while now that she'd rather I stay home for a few years while our baby is growing. I love my family, but I don't think I can spend every waking moment here."

It was all starting to add up. Richard was a model of a man physically, and those good looks had bought him one of the richest brides in Savannah. Of course, having a wealthy and beautiful wife didn't always add up to a happy life.

Matthew shifted his feet on two concrete diamonds, looking like he was trying to avoid the grass in between, as though it was a lawn he shouldn't be stepping on. "What exactly are you trying to hide from your wife?"

Richard bit his lip. "I love her, I do. But I've always had a kind of...insatiable appetite."

Oh no...Charli had a feeling she knew exactly what this man was leading to, and she had to fight the need to step a few more inches away. She needed him to confirm her suspicions, though, so she lifted her chin and smiled. "An insatiable appetite for what?"

Heat rose to Richard's face. "My love life with my wife hasn't been so easy since the baby arrived. And I...I needed something more."

Charli could've jumped out of her skin. Was he about to say it? Had he been having an affair with Candace? Had Charli finally found a romantic interest of their victim? Or was this revelation going to be even darker? Suddenly, Charli found herself praying he wasn't about to tell her he fondled dead bodies at the morgue.

"But I never cheated on her." The finality in Richard's voice signaled either that he was lying about an affair or Charli was way off base.

Charli cleared her throat. "I don't understand. If you weren't cheating, why were you at the funeral home?"

"Detective, my wife's father is an engineer. She has access to some of the best cyber security programs money can buy. She knows my every move here. So, if I want to watch porn, I have to do it somewhere else." The color heightened in his cheeks, and he pushed his glasses up on his nose.

Matthew pulled his lips inward, and Charli recognized the expression. Matthew coughed in his hand to cover up the chuckle he couldn't suppress. "You're telling me you drove all the way to your workplace to watch porn?"

"I know how it sounds. But that's the truth. This is a rather awkward confession, but what the hell? I certainly don't want anyone to think I had something to do with Candace going missing." He sucked in a breath before releasing it slowly. "There is a cam girl I really like who only comes on late at night. I like to go see her when I can. It's not healthy, and I'm working on it. But it's the truth. I can give you access to my accounts if you need proof. They'll show you what time I was online."

Matthew bit down on his lip hard. "Yeah, we're definitely going to need to take you up on that. But before we do, is there anything else you've been hiding from us?"

"Uh, like what?" Richard ran a hand over his shirt buttons, fiddling with the black button closest to his chest.

But Charli had some leverage now. "You've got a secret, Mr. Godfrey, and we're happy to keep it, but it would be supremely helpful if you could help us out as well."

Richard groaned. "Okay, I have no idea what happened to Candace, but I might know more about her personal life than I was letting on. I didn't want to say anything because I rarely saw Candace. But a couple different times, during one of my, er...late-night visits, I saw her come into the funeral home with Elwood or Jacob. Never both at the same time. And I didn't see anything beyond that."

"And you never saw her at the funeral home with Cobb?" Charli yanked her notebook out of her jacket.

"No. But I know that they had a fling way back when. Or, at least, that was the rumor around the office. I certainly didn't see anything myself."

This was useful. Finally, someone had actually seen

Candace with one of the men in the office. Charli finished writing and fixed her gaze on Richard. "And you're sure that is all you know about Candace?"

"One thing I meant when we spoke earlier was that I try to stay out of office drama. So, yes, that is all that I know." Richard held up a hand. "Now, please, please don't mention this to anyone. I can't get fired from this job because if I do, Alexandria is never going to let me go job hunt for another one."

"Your secret is safe with us, Mr. Godfrey. And we really appreciate your cooperation and your honesty." Despite his previous lies, Charli didn't clock Richard as particularly untrustworthy.

He was just a man with a secret. In Charli's experience, most men had one, and most of them would lie to a detective to protect it. She didn't hold a grudge against Richard for hiding his filthy habit, but she didn't mind leveraging his dirty secret against him if necessary.

Besides, he'd just given her an excellent lead. Candace had been spending time with both Jacob and Elwood in the off-hours of the funeral home. Charli didn't know what they were doing, but she was going to find out.

"I've got just one more question for you." Charli studied Richard's reaction. "Do you know a Marco DeStasio?"

Richard's eyes lit up. "Oh, of course. Marco has come in a few times to talk to the Kirklands."

And there it was. Now the once seemingly random stranger on the street was attached to the case. Charli had been right all along. He wasn't a random passerby who had been spooked by her and driven off. He was somehow involved in the funeral home.

The words came speeding out of Charli's mouth. "Talk to the Kirklands about what?"

"He wanted to buy the funeral home. In fact, I think it

was Candace who introduced him to the Kirklands as a potential investor. From what I heard, he offered them a pretty hefty amount for the home too."

Maybe Charli was about to get a big break in the case after all.

22

Charli averted her gaze from the stark-naked woman who dominated the computer screen.

"Well, the man wasn't lying about his porn addiction. That's for sure." Jake Taylor, the cyber security expert, suppressed a giggle.

Matthew expelled a slow sigh. "This must be the cam girl he's so obsessed with, but can we identify the times when he watched her?"

Jake leaned back in his chair, Matthew and Charli hovering over his shoulders. "I don't know. That all depends on the site. I can see if they time stamp login times, but a lot of these types of websites don't. User privacy is better for their bottom line. They don't need nosy spouses digging into the details of their partners' history. It's bad for business. But I'll see what we've got in user settings."

Charli couldn't blame Alexandria for not allowing her husband to take part in these sorts of activities. There was something disgusting about a man virtually talking to another woman sexually while his wife was at home taking care of their baby. Richard had said he'd never cheated on his wife, but Charli failed to see how this didn't constitute cheating.

Jake pointed to the computer. "I can't see when he's logged in, but I can see the time when he spent coins on different cam girls."

"Coins?" Was Charli supposed to know what that meant?

"It's how men tip the women on the site. And here is your night in question. Looks like he was indeed tipping this cam star the night in question. The alibi checks out."

There was a knock on the doorframe, and another cyber security employee, one Charli didn't recognize, popped his head in. "You sure you don't need any more help on this one?"

"Get out of here, perv." Jake threw a wadded-up piece of paper at his head. It hit him square between the eyes.

"All right, all right."

So, evidently, word had traveled about Richard Godfrey's...situation. So much for keeping his secret. But at least the guys at the precinct wouldn't tell his wife or boss.

Not a minute after the first guy popped in, yet another cyber security tech came by.

"I heard you had a very interesting case. Need any help?" He shuffled toward the computer, his eyes about to bulge out of his head.

Was this really that entertaining? If the cyber boys were so desperately interested in this case, surely they could head home to their own computers and get the content they were craving so badly.

Off the damn clock.

Jake minimized the computer screen and glanced over his shoulder. "No, man. We've got it all under control in here."

Charli rolled her eyes so hard they hurt. Jake's department was one hell of a boys' club, but it was nice that he remained so professional.

In fact, Charli wished she could share his professionalism because, when a third man came in to generously "offer his help," she about lost her mind.

"Excuse me?" Charli slammed her notebook on the desk. The poor guy with the thick-rimmed glasses flinched. "Can't you see we're investigating a very serious case? Are you all really so obsessed with a nude woman that you have to keep barging in one by one?"

He shifted his glasses up over the bridge of his nose. "Uh, actually, I was coming in to ask Jake if he could help me with a project he's working on when he's done."

Heat crept into Charli's cheeks. "Oh, right, uh…I'm sorry."

Jake and Matthew were snickering behind her, but Jake stopped long enough to answer his colleague. "Sure, Artie. I'll be right over."

Artie didn't need an excuse to scurry out of the room.

Charli didn't give a flip if anyone blamed her for her meltdown. She'd had a hell of a week, and the parade of horny guys was only delaying progress on their case.

Although Matthew and Jake were staring at her with grins on their faces, she ignored them. "Any chance you could search his computer for any mention of Candace Redding, Jacob Pernell, or Elwood Sanders?"

Jake swiveled around in his chair. "Sure thing. I'll get right on that for you."

Charli was doubtful anything useful could be found, but since Godfrey had handed over his computer willingly, there was no reason not to check it out.

She was grateful she didn't have to be the one to go through the computer. It was getting late, and this had been one hell of a day. When Charli believed Richard Godfrey would be the next big break in the case, she'd been more than happy to continue working. The drive to finish this case consumed her.

But it no longer looked like that would happen any time soon. Charli needed time to process the letter and create a plan for getting back on Madeline's case. Perhaps she could start looking into the old files while waiting for Ruth's permission. That way, she'd be ready to hit the ground running.

"Everything okay?" Matthew's footsteps were close behind Charli as she made her way down the hall.

Charli rubbed the back of her neck. "Oh, yeah. Just really tired. You're ready to head home, right?"

Matthew yawned, stretching his arms out to his sides. "Yeah. But I think we should make a plan for if and when the hair comes back from Cobb's car. If it proves to be Candace's hair, we should stake out his place."

Typically, Charli was the one jumping the gun to come up with their next plan, but she didn't have the energy. "Right. That's a good idea." Charli's words came out slower than she'd intended.

Matthew didn't carry on the conversation. Perhaps he realized that Charli was only half there, her mind drifting to another place. Or maybe his own exhaustion had taken over. They'd been hard at work on this case, starting early every morning. And Charli knew Matthew often stayed up late, regardless of how early he had to get up. He was probably more tired than she was.

But once they were about five minutes away from his home, Charli was hit with the sudden urge to break the silence. "How are things with Chelsea?"

Matthew rubbed his tired eyes. "Nothing new to report, unfortunately. But I'm still hopeful about some of your suggestions. I'm just so swamped with this case, ya know?"

Charli kept her eyes on the road in front of her. "Well, you can't let the case take over your life. You've got to take some time for yourself."

Matthew let out a chuckle. "You're one to talk, Charli."

"Actually, I'm going to take some time for myself. You remember my friend, Rebecca? We're going out for drinks."

Out of the corner of her eye, Charli glimpsed a smile that lit up Matthew's face. "Hey, that's great, Charli! And now maybe I can finally get you to come out for a drink with me."

Charli returned the grin. "We'll see about that. I'm really looking forward to hanging out with her."

A sigh escaped Charli's lips. Although it was easier said than done, she had to take her own advice and start taking some time for herself.

And she planned to start right now.

23

It wasn't hard for Charli to find Rebecca at the bar, two glasses of red wine in hand. Her friend's sparkling black blazer shone under the lights above. It matched the glitter in her eyes. She always had a gleam, like a child does when they're excited about a field trip. But for Rebecca, the field trip was life, and she was ready to live it.

How Charli wished she could attain that level of naivete, or maybe Rebecca wasn't naïve. Regardless, she was always so positive about the world around her. After everything Charli had seen on the job, she could never view the world that way.

"Charli, hey! I'm so glad you texted. I wasn't sure you wanted to hang out again since so many weeks had passed after we last met up."

From someone else, Charli might have assumed that comment was a passive-aggressive nudge about how she had ignored her friend for weeks. But from Rebecca's bubbly grin, Charli knew that wasn't what she intended.

"Yeah, sorry about that, but it's the nature of the job. Sometimes, I'm tied up for weeks on end."

Charli pulled up a chair next to Rebecca. Her beige button-down blouse with slacks faded into the background next to Rebecca's sparkling attire, though Charli might fade into the background even if Rebecca was dressed in a paper bag. Her magenta lips popped against perfect white teeth. She had a perfectly symmetrical face, with large apple cheeks. It was no surprise that Bryce Mowery chased her before his untimely death.

"Oh, of course! I can't imagine having a career so exciting. If I was a detective, I wouldn't see anyone. It would be like living in an episode of *Forensic Files*."

Charli laughed as she took the glass from Rebecca. "Well, it's not always all that exciting, although there's been a lot of drama in my life lately."

Rebecca's shapely eyebrows popped up. "Oh, drama, you say? Well, spill, girl."

Should she, though? Did Charli want to talk to Rebecca about the letter she'd received? Perhaps it would be nice to be able to talk to someone who actually knew Madeline.

Charli cleared her throat. "Did you realize that the ten-year anniversary of Madeline's death is coming up?"

Rebecca's face fell. "I did notice that, yeah. I'm so sorry, Charli, but is that still stressing you out? I mean this in the nicest way possible, but I hope you've been able to move on in a healthy way."

If Charli was being honest, yes, Madeline's death still caused her immense pain. And perhaps that wasn't the healthiest situation. She wasn't going to get into that with Rebecca, though.

"It's not that. It's just…I got a letter from the person who may have killed her. He asked me if I had given up on finding him after ten years."

Rebecca gasped, her hand flinging to her glossy lips. She

downed the rest of her glass and flagged the bartender over to request another one.

Charli sipped her own wine. "I'm sorry, that was a lot to spring on you."

Rebecca held up a hand. "No, no, it's fine. I'm glad you told me. It's just a lot to take in. But, I mean, if it's overwhelming for me, I can't imagine what it must be like for you."

Overwhelming was an understatement. That letter brought up such a mountain of emotion Charli couldn't begin to climb over the rage, shame, guilt, and sadness. She missed Madeline more than anything in this world. And to hold that much love in her heart, but to have no answers about her death...it killed Charli every time she thought about it.

So, the only answer to avoid this pain was to not think about it. And that was what Charli did most days. Occasionally, this felt like a betrayal to Madeline's memory. But, for the most part, she focused on her cases, on her friendship with Matthew, on her relationship with her dad, and she didn't do much else.

It was impossible to ignore things now, though. This letter was a concrete reminder of Madeline.

Rebecca put her hand on Charli's shoulder. She didn't know that Charli loathed being touched as a form of comfort, but Charli didn't want to interrupt the moment by telling her that.

"You know it wasn't ever your job to find him, right?"

Charli's head snapped up to meet Rebecca's gaze. It wasn't what she was expecting Rebecca to say.

"Why do you say that?" The words fumbled out of Charli's mouth as she straightened her blazer.

"You were a kid, Charli. I know you're a detective now, so it probably stings a lot that, if you were on her case back then, you could have done something about it. But it doesn't change anything."

It was as if Rebecca had seen right into her soul. Was Charli that easy to read?

She was too stunned to answer, so Rebecca continued. "It's like if your parent dies of a heart attack when you're sixteen, and then you become a doctor in your twenties. It would be ridiculous to think back and say, 'If only I was a doctor back then, I could have helped them.'"

When she put it like that, yeah, it sounded ridiculous, but that was exactly the situation Charli had been playing in her mind over and over again. She thought she could look back over Madeline's case as an experienced detective and make a breakthrough.

The truth was, only one percent of cold cases were solved. And, yes, maybe if Charli had been in charge of the case from the beginning, she would have done things differently. Perhaps she would have discovered something the original detectives hadn't.

But there was no point in wondering about that now.

Charli tucked a short lock of hair behind her ear. "It's just so hard to let go of the hope that I might someday know the truth. And what are you, a psychologist or something? You're a good friend, Becca."

A smile tugged at Rebecca's lips. "Actually, I'm a pediatric counselor. And I know what you mean, but sometimes, life doesn't wrap things up in a nice bow for us. We don't always get to know. What I do know is that Madeline loved you, and you loved her. That is no mystery, and those last moments of her life were so short compared to the infinite number of good memories you two shared."

After all these years, Charli never thought someone could say something to shift her view about Madeline's death. But this was the first time that she considered she might have been putting too much importance on the last bit of Madeline's life.

Yes, it was horrifying to think about how torturous her final moments were. But those final moments amounted to such a small piece of her life. Was it any more important than the many summers they'd spent together? The nights they stayed up late, confessing deep secrets?

Charli raised her glass. "To Madeline. To the way she lived every moment like it could be her last."

Rebecca's cheeks pinked up as she lifted her own glass high. "That's the spirit! Let's hope we can follow in her footsteps."

Something sank in Charli's chest yet again. She let her hand fall. "I don't know if I've been doing a great job of that lately."

Rebecca twisted in her stool, the soft fabric of her slacks helping her to slide effortlessly over the leather seat. "How do you mean?"

"I mean...Madeline was always pushing me to get out of my head. She wanted me to relax. I don't think a day went by when she didn't remind me not to take myself too seriously. But in her absence, that's all I've done. Madeline pulled out a lightness in me. Now my life is just...so heavy."

Charli averted her gaze from Rebecca. Such an intimate confession was difficult, and she couldn't believe she'd allowed herself to be so honest about her feelings. She gazed around the décor of the Red Rose Bar and Grill. Along the wall were retro alcohol posters. Some seemed to date back to the prohibition era, which made sense because the bar did have a speakeasy vibe. But were any of those posters authentic, or were they only designed to appear retro by some graphic design major selling Etsy prints?

"It's never too late, you know." Rebecca's words pulled Charli from her reverie. "You can start today, right now. You can find ways to honor Madeline's memory and everything she used to do for you. Maybe that's a better way to keep her in your heart, as opposed to hunting down her murderer."

Charli allowed herself to look back at Rebecca. Her ball-shaped cheeks were still lit up with a smile, though now it was more subdued. Not filled with pity, necessarily. No, Rebecca's smile held more empathy than pity. And it actually provided Charli with a modicum of comfort.

Charli stared at the red liquid swirling around in her glass. "I just don't know. How do I bring her back into my world?"

Charli had allowed Madeline to become a ghost when she wanted nothing more in the world than to bring her back to life.

Rebecca put both hands on Charli's shoulders. Until that moment, Charli hadn't seen that even Rebecca's nails had a light-colored shimmering coat. Now, Charli was absorbed in the glitter that sat on her shoulder as Rebecca gave her a little shake.

"Come on now, Charli. Madeline is all around you all the time. You just have to look for her. Here, turn to that empty chair. Imagine she's sitting next to you. What would she say to you now?"

Charli bit her lip as she swiveled to the empty chair. It felt silly, picturing her body there. But she closed her eyes and, when she opened them, Madeline's familiar face was smiling back at her. She still had the little gap in her front teeth. To this day, Charli found herself disarmed by anyone with a similar gap.

"Charli, what are you doing?" Madeline's voice echoed in her mind. It was as real as the day she'd disappeared. Charli could never forget the high-pitched squeak that came out when Madeline was asking a particularly dramatized question.

But Charli didn't know. She had no idea what she was doing.

"Do you think I want you to avenge me? Because I don't. It's already sucky enough to die as a teenager, but to watch my best friend spend her entire life obsessed with the fact that I'm gone? I don't want that for you! I want you to have a life! I want you to go out on dates, see friends, take a vacation."

But for ten years, Charli had ignored all those facets of her life. All she had to show romantically was a long train of hook-ups that never amounted to anything. Her only close friend was the man she worked with. And not once had she ever taken a vacation, though it would be easy enough to pull the funds from her savings.

"Live your damn life, Charli. Because you have one. God knows I'd be living mine even if you were the one who kicked the bucket."

Charli had to chuckle out loud at that, which made her fear someone was about to throw her in the looney bin for laughing at a voice that wasn't there. But when she glanced back at Rebecca, her gentle hazel eyes showed no judgment.

"See? Isn't that nice?"

It was. It really was nice to hear Madeline again. And though it wasn't real, it felt like exactly what Madeline would say to her.

Charli was in no position to be planning a vacation with her work schedule, and she certainly couldn't grab another date right now. But there was one thing on Madeline's list that Charli could make a priority.

"Rebecca, can we do this more often? I mean, I can't promise to make it out every week with my work schedule. But I'd love to have a standing date for us to meet up if that's something you'd be interested in."

Rebecca's smile stretched so far Charli thought the tips of her lips might touch her ears. "Are you kidding? Yes! I'd love to! Anytime you can see me, Charli, I'll be there, as long as you promise to tell me a few juicy detective details now and then."

Though Charli couldn't talk about active cases, she could always scrounge up some details from cases that had long gone to trial. "I think I can make that work."

If Madeline was still around, like Rebecca claimed, Charli knew she'd be happy to see this.

24

I surveyed the ramshackle building in front of me. Was this it? The run-down motel barely had a sign outside. But this had to be the location. The boss said it was the motel across from Payter's Grill. I could barely make out the letters on the dilapidated sign. *Pilbo's Motel? Bilbo's Motel?* Maybe that was it.

So, this was where that little asshole had been hiding out. My job would be a whole lot easier if the people would just accept they were as good as dead already. Didn't they know when they made my list, I was going to get to them no matter what?

Not that I disliked the chase. The hunt was often as good as the thrill of the kill, and none of these little rodents would ever get away.

I parked in the back of the lot, far off enough that it was unlikely I would be noticed. With a caution that came with years of experience, I exited my vehicle and surveyed the building. From where I had parked, I could view every entrance. Excellent. Satisfied with my traipse around the motel, I settled back into my car.

Motels were so damn depressing. They made me think of childhood road trips. I hadn't been in one since before I turned eighteen. Now, nobody could even catch me in a Hilton. It was five stars or nothing.

And I wouldn't degrade myself by getting a motel room like this bozo, not even to avoid death. I'd face someone like the man I was before I got a cheap room in a sleazeball place like this. The man wasn't just cowardly. He was prideless.

I glanced around for his car in the parking lot, but there wasn't one. So, the idiot was smart enough to ditch or hide his car. He must really be out here thinking I wasn't going to find him.

But he didn't know me too well, then. I always found my target.

I pulled out a bag of sunflower seeds from my glove compartment. There was no way to know how long this kind of mission would last. When someone was truly terrified, they could stay holed up in a room an extraordinarily long time.

And it wasn't like I could go knocking from door to door. As soon as he heard a knock, he'd know I had found him. Not that him knowing made my job impossible, but it made it more difficult. I wasn't really looking for a difficult day. The easier my job was, the better for me.

Waiting around, I was used to. There was a kind of peace surrounding the act, actually. Waiting for a victim to come out of hiding was kind of like my "me time." Once I finished with this, it would be on to the next task. Might as well slow down and run out the clock a bit.

A sunflower seed snapped against my two molars, throttling toward my cheek. I spit it out into a nearby fast-food cup that held the soda from my last meal.

I wasn't sure how long I'd been out there before I finally caught a glimpse of him, maybe an hour or so. But when I saw that shaggy head of hair pop out of room thirteen, my heart nearly soared out of my chest.

Though, for a moment, I was thrown off by the blond hair. Not just blond but bleached nearly white. It wasn't the first time I'd seen that color. Plenty of victims thought a box of bleach was enough to disguise themselves. But this wasn't Hannah Montana. A bit of blond wasn't gonna fool anyone.

I pulled out the Polaroid from the glove compartment and glanced between it and the man standing on the balcony before me, shakily taking out a cigarette and lighter. Oh, that was him, all right. There was no mistaking him. He had the same pointy chin, hollow cheekbones, and Dumbo elephant ears.

Something was distinctly different about him, though, and it wasn't just his horrible dye job. His eyes were more sunken. Nervous hands fidgeted with his lighter before running through his burnt-out strands of hair. The man had been holed up and terrified for days.

Well, that was no way to live, and I was here to help. I'd be able to put him out of his misery.

I reached for my gun in the console. I'd wait until he went back into the room, and then a "janitor" would make an unexpected house call. Unfortunately, the real custodial staff was going to have quite the mess to take care of. I'd leave a tip for them. One thing I never liked to do was inconvenience innocent bystanders. Not my style.

When his cigarette was nearly burnt to a crisp, I knew it was almost time to make my move. With one hand on the car door handle and the other on my weapon, I heard the screech of sirens, and they were headed my way.

That was the only sound that could send the hair on the back of my neck shooting up, but I couldn't afford to let the fear soaking into my spine cloud my judgment.

I always knew this moment could come. In my line of

work, one didn't always make it to retirement. One day, the law would catch up to me. I just wasn't expecting today to be the day.

But no matter. If I was going to go out, I'd go out guns blazing, literally. I pulled a second gun from my glove compartment and watched the cop cars pour in.

One.

Then two.

Then three cars?

They had to send three cop cars, each with two pigs just to come get me? Well, that was quite the compliment. But it wasn't going to help. Six cops, one of me. I didn't hate those odds. Cops always thought they knew their way around a weapon, but they didn't. Most cops had never had to shoot at an actual person before.

But I'd built my career on eliminating human targets. There was no doubt in my mind I was a better shot than these bozos. And maybe if I could get them all quick, I'd have a chance to make a run for it. It would finally be off to Mexico for me.

Even if I couldn't get out of this, though, I'd face it like a man. I wouldn't be like that coward up there, holed up in a motel room, crying my eyes out about my impending doom. My only regret was I could no longer take that asshole out.

I was on the edge of my seat, waiting for the cop cars to surround me, but they didn't. I remained at the back of the lot while they parked directly in front of the motel.

They weren't here for me at all. They'd come for him.

Relief morphed into irritation.

If I'd been able to get to him just half an hour earlier, this would've been fine. But the fact that this prick was still alive could threaten our entire operation.

Dammit.

The boss was not going to be happy. I picked up my phone and dialed his number.

"Is it done?" There was no emotion behind the greeting.

"I'm afraid not. Before I had a chance to…eliminate him, they got him. The cops got Elwood."

25

After meeting Rebecca for drinks, Charli was in a pensive mood. Rarely did she ever feel lonely in her house, but it felt oddly hollow at the moment. Madeline's ghost lingered somehow, her memory permeating every room.

Charli had spent a lot of time at her grandmother's house growing up, which meant Madeline spent many days here too. They'd played with dolls in the living room in elementary school, chasing each other up and down the stairs to play tag. In their teenage years, they'd slept over in the guest bedroom and stayed up late, whispering secrets to each other long into the night.

Charli had lived in this house alone for many years now, so these memories didn't usually weigh her down. But they were an anchor on her heart now, and she desperately needed something to distract herself.

After halfheartedly picking at a microwaved dinner, she reached for the phone to dial Madeline's mother. During their last call, it didn't seem she was doing so well. While Charli had the time, she wanted to check in.

"Charlotte, is that you?"

A soft smile settled on Charli's lips as she heard her friend's mother's voice. "It's me."

"You know, your caller ID still shows up under your grandmother's name. You should get that changed, sweetheart."

Normally, Charli hated to be called pet names like "sweetheart." It was condescending and slightly sexist. She was a grown woman, but Madeline's mother had been calling her "sweetheart" since she was seven years old. Out of her mouth, there was no condescension.

"Yeah, I'll get that done soon." But Charli knew she wouldn't. She was far too busy with work to worry about the name on her caller ID. Plus, she appreciated the anonymity it provided.

"I'm glad you called, though. To what do I owe the pleasure?"

As Marcia spoke, Charli couldn't believe she'd let so many years pass without being in contact with this woman. She'd always been a second mother to her. Now that her own mother had passed away from cancer, she was the only mom Charli had.

"I just wanted to check in on you. I know with the anniversary coming up, things are hard." For a moment, Charli considered telling her about the letter.

But no, that would be far too cruel. She barely had the capacity to deal with the anniversary. Hearing about the letter was either going to terrify her or give her hope. What if the news of the letter pushed Marcia over the edge? Either way, it would be an unkindness. Unless Charli could find something concrete, she wouldn't bring it up.

A soft sigh drifted through the phone. "Oh, did I worry you? I'm sorry. I know I had a bit of a breakdown during our last call, but I'm fine, really. I've been much better since then."

There was a quiver to her voice. Charli doubted very much that she was fine, but should she press it? Obviously, this was a touchy subject.

Charli chose to move on. "It was really nice being able to reminisce with you. Another memory of Madeline came to me recently, and I thought you might want to hear it."

"I'd love to, dear."

Charli reached for a kitchen chair and pulled it over to her. She'd been leaning against the wall, and exhaustion was beginning to sink in. "Do you remember how Madeline and I used to spend our summers at that community pool?"

Charli went on to tell her how Madeline taught her to float by first teaching her about relaxation. Of course, she didn't mention why this buried memory had bubbled up to the surface.

"Oh, that's just like Madeline, isn't it? That girl was able to let all her worries go in the blink of an eye. I used to worry, actually, about what kind of adult she'd turn out to be."

Charli propped her elbows on the wooden table. "Really? How so?" Charli had never considered such a thing. Of course, she wasn't Madeline's mother, so why would she?

"Well, being an adult comes with a lot of stress and logistics. That girl kept her head so far up in the clouds, she couldn't ground herself even if she wanted to. Imagine Madeline with some boring office job, having to pay her bills on time every month while keeping a household together."

Madeline wouldn't have had some boring old office job. Charli knew that much. As for keeping a household? Even at sixteen, Madeline couldn't even keep her bed made. Her room was an assortment of clothing piles and school folders jammed with old homework.

Charli smiled into the phone. "I'm sure she would've been late on quite a few of those bills."

There was a chuckle from the other end of the line.

"Exactly. She was a fun-loving child, and a free-spirited teenager, but it's hard to picture her as an adult, perhaps because she wasn't ever meant to become one."

A darkness settled over their conversation. Charli didn't know what the appropriate answer to this was. Agreeing that the universe never intended for Madeline to reach adulthood was a depressing thought, but maybe this thought was actually a comfort to a grieving mother. Charli could argue that, though Madeline was a bit of a mess, she would've done fine as an adult. After all, Charli wasn't so great at housekeeping herself, and a utility bill occasionally slipped through the cracks.

In her heart, Charli actually believed Madeline would've made a fine adult. She was a free spirit, yes, but plenty of adults were. Madeline was also scrappy, and she would've done whatever she needed to in order to survive.

Would saying this hurt more, though? It was painful for Charli to entertain the idea of the kind of person Madeline could have become. She didn't imagine it was any easier for her mother.

Charli twirled the phone cord around her finger. "Well, that free spirit always managed to keep me from obsessing too much. These days, I could really use that."

"Then find it, sweetheart. Go get a massage. Take a long walk in Madeline's honor. Do something for yourself. She would love that."

There wasn't even time in Charli's schedule for a short walk, let alone a massage. But it was getting late, and she didn't want to keep Marcia up any longer. After agreeing to find a way to chill out, she said her goodbyes.

Charli didn't have a clue how to start relaxing, though. And at the moment, she really needed to. Waves of stress rolled over her as soon as she hung up the phone. Thoughts about the letter and her case swirled around in her mind. She wasn't entirely ready to head up to bed. Were there any chores she needed to do?

Of course there were. With how busy Charli was at her job, she was always neglecting housework. A better question was, where should she begin? Charli slipped out of her jacket and hung it on the coatrack near the door, glimpsing the wire metal basket that her grandma had hung up to place incoming mail. When was the last time Charli had checked the mail, anyway?

She would start with that. One time, she'd let the mail go for an entire month and ended up having to go to the post office to collect it as her mailbox became too full. The post office was on the other side of town, so the trip was a huge hassle, and Charli would rather not deal with it again.

The cool night air permeated the darkness. Charli took in the breeze that tussled her short hair. When she pulled open the squeaky mailbox door, a piece of white paint chipped off the edge. Charli was damn lucky she didn't live in a neighborhood with an HOA. The violations that would accumulate on this old house would be sky-high.

She allowed herself to linger on the way back up to the porch as she flipped through what was mostly junk mail. But between the flyers for local businesses, Charli's fingers paused on a smooth white envelope.

Charli's heart leapt into her throat. The air rushed from her lungs, threatening to suffocate her. But she wouldn't allow the shock of yet another white envelope to render her useless.

She sprang into action, scanning the smooth white enclosure for information.

There was no return address, and the postage showed this letter was from Greensboro, just like the one she'd received earlier.

The world began to spin around her again, and Charli

was desperate to stave off the all too familiar feeling. She had to ground herself. She couldn't jump to conclusions. Perhaps this wasn't what she thought it was.

That was when an odd detail stuck out to her. Her name was written by hand on the front of the envelope, but it was in a different handwriting than the letter she'd read earlier. She would know. Those words were carved into her memory like initials on a tree stump. There was no getting those words out of her mind.

Still, even considering the different handwriting, Charli rarely received handwritten letters. What were the chances she had received not one but two in one day?

She had to treat this more delicately. With the first letter, she had no idea what she was about to open. But now that she had an inkling of what this envelope could entail, she sprinted to her car to get a pair of gloves. No way was she going to touch the inside of this envelope with her bare hands.

Charli rushed into the house and snapped the gloves on her wrists before very carefully tearing the edge of the envelope, preserving the outside as much as possible.

The white paper fell onto the black granite of her kitchen countertops. It was folded into thirds, and Charli's hands inched the edges of the paper open.

Like the last, this letter was short and sweet. It contained only a few sentences.

And to think...if we'd gotten you that day, along with your friend, you wouldn't be worrying about all of this. What a heavy burden it must be.

We?

And just like that, Charli's world fell to pieces again. She dropped the letter on the countertop before she crashed to the floor. Every muscle in her body shook underneath her.

What the hell did that even mean? Were there really two

people who were involved in killing Madeline? Charli had never pursued the possibility there was more than one killer because she'd only seen one man grab Madeline. Nobody had been in the passenger seat of the van.

Or had there been? That day was a blur. She had been more fixated on the license plate, which ended up being pointless since it was a fake. Had she even looked in the passenger window? Was it possible that Charli might have missed such a crucial detail?

Nausea overwhelmed her senses, and she raced to the bathroom, flinging up the toilet lid to avoid having her vomit cascading on the tile. She made it just in time. Heaving stomach spasms sent the contents of her dinner into the toilet bowl.

Charli hadn't been sick like this since her last stomach flu a few years back. Sweat beaded on her forehead, and when she was finished, she collapsed onto the floor. The cool tile against her cheek soothed her burning skin.

What the hell was happening? Why now? Why would she be getting these letters now? Charli found herself praying that Ruth was right, that this was just someone messing with her, because the alternative was too much to bear.

Charli had only barely survived the guilt of Madeline being taken right before her eyes. She would never forgive herself if she had failed to notice a second person at the scene. Searching for two killers would have changed the entire investigation. That was a huge revelation.

And another huge revelation slammed into Charli like a pile of bricks. Whoever had sent that letter, whether they were a killer or simply someone who wanted to cause her distress, knew where she lived. This wasn't addressed to the precinct. They had been able to find her house.

Charli unholstered her gun as she scrambled to her feet. Her skin was slick with sweat, her legs continuing to tremble. But she had to wrestle with her discomfort because sweeping her house of anyone dangerous was her top priority. She didn't have the luxury of a mental breakdown.

Years of training kicked in, and she went room by room, kicking doors in swiftly and peeking into every closet. She checked every nook and cranny of her house but found nothing.

Charli expected that. After all, the letter hadn't been hand-delivered. It had postage from Greensboro. But she couldn't be too careful.

Charli was about ready to collapse and wallow once more, when her cell phone rang from her pocket. Matthew was calling.

"W-what's going on?" The stutter surprised even Charli, but her partner didn't question it.

"I know we said we were done for the day, but I've got something that might change your mind."

Charli let her shoulders fall. She hadn't even realized they'd been so tense. Of course, the only thing that could dissipate that tension would be a break in the case.

She blew out the breath she'd been holding. "What is it?"

"State officers have found Elwood. He's in custody now."

A smile crept onto Charli's lips, despite the chaos of her current predicament. "Then let's go have a conversation with him."

26

Charli had bagged the envelope and brought it with her to the precinct, but she didn't tell Matthew about it yet. Her priority was to get it checked for prints, but she wasn't ready to talk about the ramifications of the letter's contents. And if she told Matthew, he'd tell Ruth, and the sergeant would most likely suggest that she needed some time away from work.

Spending time away from work would only send Charli spiraling. The last thing she wanted was to sit at home and let her mind race. Here at work, she was useful. Back at home, her feelings of uselessness would send her into a black hole of despair.

Charli stood outside of the interrogation room as a nervous Elwood traced the lines of his palms. Matthew opened the door behind her.

"I talked to Ruth and let her know where we're at. You ready to go in there?"

Was she ever. "Let's do it."

Elwood already had a water bottle in front of him that he hadn't touched. If he was too nervous to drink water, that was a good sign. In Charli's experience, a suspect was easier to crack when they showed outward symptoms of anxiety.

Charli let a few moments of silence go by before she spoke, ramping up the pressure. "Hi, Mr. Sanders. I'm Detective Cross, and this is my partner, Detective Church. We'll be recording our conversation today." She followed protocol and said the time and date for the recording before getting down to business. "I'm going to start by asking you when you last saw Candace Redding."

Elwood's fingers dug even further into his palm. He did not make eye contact. "I don't know. A week ago, maybe. I can't remember."

Matthew stared on at him, although the man didn't return their gaze. "How about Jacob Pernell?"

"Probably the same. Sometime at work a week ago. I don't know." Elwood gave an upward jerk of his shoulders, as if this wasn't terribly important.

"Are you sure?" Charli tapped her finger against the metal table. "Because you sure look like you know something. Are you bothered by being here?"

"I'm in a police station. Of course I'm bothered." Elwood's voice was a near whisper. His pale pink lips barely moved as he spoke.

Although his answers were short, there was no confidence behind his words. Charli grew more and more sure they'd be able to crack him tonight. "Why'd you leave town, Mr. Sanders?"

There was a slight shake of Elwood's head, causing his bleached blond hair to wave from side to side. "I don't know. I was just sick of Savannah. I needed a break."

Matthew chuckled. "Is the dye job for us?"

It wasn't unusual for a perp to dye their hair in an effort to evade the police. Although, usually, when someone was trying to escape the law, they made plans to leave the country as soon as possible. According to the state officers, Elwood had been found just forty minutes outside of Savannah. Since it had been nearly a week since he told his roommate he might not be back, he could've been out of the country by now. The detectives knew he had a valid passport.

Charli sucked in a deep breath as she remembered their interview with Jacob Pernell. Maybe Elwood didn't want to leave the country because it wasn't the law he feared. Maybe the bleach job wasn't for them at all.

She took a sharp turn in her questioning. "Mr. Sanders, if you're hiding from someone, we can protect you. Hair dye isn't going to keep you safe from whoever you're running from."

Matthew glanced over at Charli, a slight squint in his eyes. She only raised one brow in response. Any communication they had in this interrogation room had to be hidden from Elwood.

"I'm not hiding from anyone." Elwood folded his arms, but the way his eyes fell to the right suggested otherwise. With his gaze downcast, he began to fumble with the worn sleeve of his shirt.

"That's good. Because whoever Jacob and Candace were hiding from, it didn't work out so well for them. I'm glad you're not on that same path. It's unfortunate, though. If Mr. Pernell had decided to come forward with everything he knew right away, he might still be alive today." Charli gave a quick shrug.

The color drained from Elwood's face. He was white as a ghost. "Yeah? What could you have done to protect him?"

"We could've taken him into our custody. Sent him to a safe house of an undisclosed location that is under constant supervision." Charli finally caught a bit of eye contact with Elwood, who had stopped tracing the lines in his hand.

Elwood bit the corner of his lip. He was silent for a

moment, and when he spoke, Charli had to strain to hear him. "But if he was in your custody, he'd be in prison."

"Not necessarily." Charli leaned forward to try to engage with him further. His interest was obvious. "To our knowledge, he hadn't done anything wrong, and if he had, we would have protected him anyway."

Matthew pulled his lips in as he gave a slow nod. "A lot of cases we've worked on have resulted in generous plea deals in exchange for pertinent information."

Elwood tossed his head into his hands, fingers clinging to both of his temples. "Oh, screw it. Fine. Even prison has got to be better than living with this constant fear. I'll tell you everything."

Cracked like an egg in a frying pan. Charli wasn't going to ask any more questions. She'd let Elwood start to tell his story first, in his own words.

"It all started a year ago. At least, it did for me. That was when Candace came to me and told me she needed help. She offered me a large sum of money to…" Elwood's cheeks reddened. Whatever he and Candace had been up to, he took no pride in it.

Charli pressed him further. "To do what?"

"At first, she told me she needed help running the cremator at night when nobody was around. I thought he just wanted to burn undesirable items. For a long time, I didn't know…" There was a catch in Elwood's voice. "I didn't know they were people."

"People?" Charli failed to hide her shock. "You and Candace were burning bodies?"

"Yes. And I wanted out when I found that out. I did. But Candace told me there was no getting out. That we were doing this for very powerful mafia connections. If I ever stopped, they'd kill me."

Charli had been open to the possibility that Candace had

been dabbling in illegal activity with all her cash deposits, but this was beyond the scope of Charli's imagination. With all the documentaries she watched and books she'd read, Charli thought she'd heard it all. But to use mortuary cremators to burn multiple bodies for the mob? That was the kind of thing Charli thought she'd only find in a work of fiction.

Matthew's eyes were nearly bulging out of his head, so he had to be thinking something similar. "And the bodies we found this past week. They were also burned up by the mafia?"

Elwood buried his head in his hands. "I honestly don't know who was in there. I can't tell you that. But I'd be lying if I said I didn't think one of those bodies belonged to Candace."

A neutral expression was pasted on Matthew's face. "Why is that?"

Rubbing a hand across his face, Elwood drew in a deep breath. "Because she was planning to ask the mafia bosses for more money. Actually, she wanted double the money for all of us. Except I didn't give a shit about that. I was already planning my escape. I knew her plan to ask for higher payments wasn't going to go well, and I wasn't about to be a part of it. These aren't the kind of guys you demand money from."

"Wait a second." Charli put a hand up to stop him. "Did you say 'all of us'?" The term implied more than just Elwood and Candace.

"Yeah, Jacob too. And Jacob was down for more money. Both of them had expensive tastes. Not me, though. I never even moved out of my crappy rental. I guess that's why it was easier for me to try and walk away. But I really didn't want more money. I just wanted to stop being involved with the damn mob. Mainly, I just don't want them to kill me."

The story was so elaborate that Charli couldn't help but

consider that Elwood might be lying. But making his cheeks flush on command couldn't be an easy task. And if he did make all of this up, he should be working as an author instead of at a funeral home.

Matthew leaned forward, studying Elwood intently. "What do you know about the men you worked for?"

"Not a lot. I really only know one of their names, and that's Marco DeStasio. And I only know that because Candace once came in with him to talk to the Kirklands about buying out the funeral home. I've met a few other guys, but they stay nameless. They never told us about the bodies we were cremating, either. None of us had any details about who they killed. They didn't want us to have information that could be used against them."

Charli's jaw dropped open. Candace absolutely had details about the bodies they'd burned. She might not have been given names, but she took extremely detailed notes of those she cremated. That was what her notebook was about. She wasn't people-watching. The secretary was recording details in case she ever needed them. Smart girl.

Well, relatively smart, anyway. Deciding to work with a mob boss wasn't so intelligent.

But thanks to Elwood, they knew exactly who that mob boss was.

And Charli was about to track him down.

27

Charli let the door to the interrogation room slam behind her. "There's no way he could be lying. Not with all the little details he'd provided."

After a lengthy questioning from Charli and Matthew, they let Elwood know the safest place for him was at the precinct. Until they could get their hands on Marco DeStasio, he was better off in custody.

"Are we sure there's no way?" Matthew scratched his head. "I mean, he knows who Marco is, but so does Richard. Anyone at the funeral home would know him."

Charli had already considered that. But, no, there were way too many aspects of this crime that had fit Elwood's scenario.

"It's not just Marco DeStasio. Think about Candace's journal. It makes perfect sense that she would be writing descriptions of bodies that disappeared. And we know she got a ton of cash deposits from an undisclosed place. This makes perfect sense. I mean, sure, he might be lying about the fact that he didn't want to be a part of it. It is hard to believe he wasn't aware these were bodies from the start. But the overarching scenario here is the first one that has made perfect sense."

A shiver went up Charli's spine as another piece of the puzzle fell together.

Matthew studied Charli's reaction. "What is it?"

She tucked a wayward lock of her short hair behind her ear. "If Elwood is right and Marco DeStasio is a mob boss, that means we're being followed by the mafia."

A silence settled over the room. If Elwood's story was true, this would be a first for both of them. Obviously, the detectives had spent their careers trying to catch murderers, but the mafia was an entirely different beast. They were an organized criminal association. And according to Elwood, this particular mob branch had managed to kill numerous people and burn their bodies without ever being caught.

Charli's face fell as her eyes glazed over, as though she was looking at something far in the distance, and internally, she was. She racked her brain, skimming through the details of Madeline's case.

Could a criminal organization have been responsible for Madeline's death? Was that why it was so hard to catch who had killed her? Hell, if that were the case, maybe more than one person had been responsible. Charli couldn't be sure.

Matthew waved a hand in front of Charli's face. "Earth to Charli?"

Crap. How long had she been in la-la land? Charli couldn't focus on Madeline's abduction right now. At the moment, she had another case at hand, and she was on the verge of solving it.

Charli flashed her partner a smile. She was back on track now.

Matthew returned her grin. "I think our next priority should be finding Marco DeStasio. For all we know, he's got connections who are working hard to find out where

Elwood is. If he knows he's in our custody, this could get ugly."

He wasn't wrong. Charli had no doubt Marco was on the hunt for Elwood. But they couldn't just head over to the mafia member's home now. "If we go to Marco without solid evidence, he's going to know we're on to him. He'll have his lawyer on us in a heartbeat, and he isn't going to say a word. Until we have a court order, we're not getting any evidence from him."

Matthew massaged his right arm and winced ever so slightly. "Right. But what other evidence can we even collect at this point? We've got Elwood's statement. That's something."

Sure, it was something. But with the kind of high-powered lawyers Marco would be hiring, having just the man's statement wasn't enough.

Lawyers like Tom Rawson. Now, at least, Charli understood a bit better how Jacob's interview at the station had gotten him killed.

That bastard attorney had mostly likely been in the mafia's pocket.

Charli racked her brain for something, anything else they could do. "We have more security footage, right?"

Matthew leaned back against the two-way mirror behind him. "Yes. But we've gone over the night in question about a million times. I doubt we're going to find anything else."

"But now we know Marco DeStasio was bringing bodies to the mortuary regularly. If we can show that he was at the funeral home after hours, we can add some validity to Elwood's statement. Plus, we have Candace's journal, with dates and times, which should help. Let's each start going through the video feeds."

Going through security footage was tedious work. Charli wasn't particularly excited about it, and she could only imagine Matthew was equally less than thrilled. Not to mention the fact that Charli was desperate to be back home, asleep in her bed.

Although, when Matthew called, she'd been a little too shaken to sleep. And that wasn't going to improve now that she knew she was investigating the mafia. Marco had been following Charli's car. How much did he know about her? Had he been outside her house?

Was he responsible for the letters?

Charli gave her head a quick shake to rid herself of the thought. Idly wondering how much danger she could be in wouldn't do her any good. What she had to prioritize was getting enough information that Marco could be arrested. That way, he couldn't harm her or anybody else.

The detectives sat in silence for the next hour as they each sat at their computers and sifted through old footage. Thankfully, the security system had been designed to alert of any motion detection, which made it easier to find the moments when someone was actually outside the funeral home. Unfortunately, the block where the funeral home was located had a gang of stray cats roaming the street.

Matthew tossed his head back. "I swear, if I see one more tabby walk across this security camera at three a.m., I'm going to scream."

"Oh, the gray cat is Leo. I named him." Charli clicked on the night prior to the one she'd been looking at and realized she was now nearly a month into her search. "Wait, how much video footage do we have, exactly?"

Matthew stifled a yawn. "I think several years. Why?"

"What kind of hard drive do you have to have to store years' worth of mundane security footage?"

"It's not on a hard drive, Charli." Matthew didn't even attempt to hide his smirk. "It's uploaded to the cloud. You know, just like all the photos and videos on your phone."

Charli needed more caffeine. "Oh, I guess you do have a point."

Although she considered herself to be tech-savvy enough, Charli just didn't have that much time to spend on her phone and computer outside of work. In that way, she was more boomer than millennial.

A thought hit Charli, and a gasp escaped her lips.

Candace was a millennial, too, probably much more tech-savvy than Charli, judging from her choice of apartment complex with a smart hub that tracked her every move.

"What is it?" Matthew kicked off the tile floor so his chair would roll closer to Charli's desk. "Did you see anything?"

Charli pushed her short bangs off her forehead. "Don't we have one of Candace's tablets in custody?"

Matthew glanced at the computer screen and back at Charli. "I believe so, but it was password protected. Cyber sec was working on a warrant to get access to her devices. Not sure if it's come through yet."

"Let me check." Charli reached for her mouse and opened her email. "Bingo…we've got the warrant. Could you get us the tablet from evidence and the warrant while you're at it? They've probably cloned it already."

Matthew inhaled a slow, deep breath. "Charli, what's going on? We were just talking about a tabby, and now you urgently want Candace's devices?"

Charli expected her partner would know how she operated by now. At any rate, she wouldn't know if her theory was right until she had Candace's device in hand. "It might be nothing. Don't get your hopes up that I'm on to something."

Matthew shrugged. "I guess I could use a break from watching late-night cat fights anyway."

When Matthew returned with the warrant and Candace's cloned tablet in hand, Charli plugged the device into the wall and opened it up.

"So, because of the cloud, this should have the same apps and content as her phone does, right?" Charli went to the camera roll and started sifting through Candace's latest photos. Most of them were flirty selfies. It wasn't too difficult to see why Jacob Pernell's wife experienced a bit of jealousy whenever Candace was involved.

Matthew rubbed one eye, the exhaustion written all over his face. "I mean, some people have different apps on different devices. But for the most part, they sync up."

There were no photos or messages from the night in question, and Charli's hopes were slowly dashed. Perhaps she had expected a little much of Candace. If she was indeed killed by the mafia on the night in question, her mind could've been going in a million different directions. Despite her journal detailing the descriptions of the bodies that had been cremated, Candace might not always have been prepared to collect evidence.

Charli frowned as she started to swipe between the pages of apps. "You know, I think I got a little ahead of myself. Unless something was erased off the cloud, which I'm sure the cyber guys will tell us if that's the case, I don't think I'm going to find anything here. I was just hoping that…"

Matthew careened his neck over to peer over Charli's shoulder. "What is it, Charli? What do you see?"

Charli swallowed hard. Above a black icon with a red circle in the middle read the word "recorder." The app was in between a huddle of other random apps. Charli's heart was a drumline in her chest.

Before clicking, she had to calm down. Why would anything be in an app like this? Wouldn't Candace have just used her camera to record video or audio?

Unless she knew the men she was with might look at her camera roll and wipe anything of interest? Maybe this seemingly benign default app was the perfect place to hide valuable information.

Before she explained anything to Matthew, Charli clicked the app. In the recorder app's library, there was only one untitled file. Charli clicked play without hesitation.

"Hurry, before someone sees you." A soft female voice spoke out from the tablet speakers.

Matthew leaned over Charli's shoulder even further. "Is that…Candace?"

But she didn't answer. She was too glued to the audio.

Just as Elwood had said, Candace proceeded to request an increase in pay. And Elwood had also been right about the fact that the mafia bosses were not going to take kindly to this.

The audio grew increasingly more and more sickening. A cluster of knots formed in the pit of Charli's stomach as she listened to Candace plead for her life. Although what she'd been doing was positively despicable, nobody deserved the death that she proceeded to receive.

Her screams were a caterwaul against the silence of the office walls. The bone-chilling screech was unlike anything Charli had ever heard. They were the shrieks of a woman who knew her impending death was coming. She'd worked a lot of vile cases, but none where there was an actual record of a victim's last moments. Charli's mind returned to the last time she'd heard a scream even half that horrifying…the day Madeline was stolen.

Though this was even worse than Madeline's scream for help. On that fateful day nearly a decade ago, Madeline still had the hope that she would make it out with her life. These were the screeches of a woman who knew she was never going to see the light of day again, the last shrieks of pain before Candace was no longer able to breathe.

When the recording was over, Charli and Matthew

remained silent for a moment, neither one of them able to move.

Matthew swallowed hard. His eyes were hollow with this new information. "I guess we have our evidence."

That was the understatement of the year. Undeniable proof of Candace's last moments, the recording was also a hint to the identity of the other victim in the cremator.

Normally, getting such a crucial piece of evidence in a case would be a joyous moment, especially a case like this, where they had minimal leads and only an inkling of what happened at the funeral home prior to talking with Elwood. In the last couple hours, they'd gone from virtually clueless to having a recording of the night in question.

But there was no joy in their office at the moment. The recording was a stark reminder of the brutality of Candace's passing. Even more so, it was a reminder of the fact that they never really *won* a case. Candace certainly hadn't won, and neither had any of the victims she'd helped dispose of.

Charli steadied her breath in order to calm the pounding in her chest, reminding herself that she still had the opportunity to prevent this from happening to anyone else. If she let herself get swept away in the horror the victims experienced, she wouldn't be able to do her job effectively.

She searched for a time stamp on the audio. It appeared to end at 1:07 in the morning on the night Candace disappeared. That was approximately the same time that her cell phone could no longer be found by local GPS trackers.

Charli massaged the back of her neck, the exhaustion settling low in her belly. "The time stamps all line up with the time Candace's phone was destroyed. The only thing left to do is get a confirmation of a witness that these are the voices of Candace and Marco DeStasio, then see if we can identify the other man involved."

Matthew leaned back in his chair, his shoulders slumping

down in the black faux leather. "Elwood should be able to do that. Then we can speak to Ruth and see how quickly we can apprehend Marco. But who was the first male voice we heard?"

Charli had been wondering the same thing. "I don't know. Maybe Elwood will be able to tell us."

The more mafia bosses Charli was able to take down with this case, the better.

28

Elwood recognized the other man in the recording, but he couldn't identify him by name. Evidently, Marco DeStasio was the only guy who allowed his name to be known due to his attempt to buy out the funeral home.

The outcome was not what Charli was hoping for, but getting DeStasio was the goal. They could do that now. Ruth was able to get in touch with the district attorney to explain that they needed to arrest Marco immediately. If they didn't, the detectives and officers who apprehended Elwood might be in danger. And, of course, Elwood himself was at great risk.

Because of the heightened threat, a team of officers was required to bring DeStasio in. Charli jumped at the opportunity to be there, but Ruth fought against it. Nobody was sure what kind of setup a man like DeStasio would have at his house. For all they knew, he was armed with weaponry and guards to do his dirty work. The sergeant had no interest in the possibility of her lead detectives being shot.

"But how will it look if Charli and I aren't there to arrest the suspect in our own case?" Matthew had argued with Ruth.

"It will look like you're letting the SWAT team do its job. And it will look like you are making the intelligent decision not to put a target on your back." Ruth pointed a finger in both of their faces. "Go home and try to get some sleep. I need you fresh in the morning."

Sleep didn't come easily for Charli.

Though she and Matthew couldn't be there, they remained in constant contact with the team that was. There were no guns drawn, mainly because the officers didn't give DeStasio enough warning to prepare any weapons. The team showed up at his house without sirens or lights, stealthily infiltrating his domain under the early morning cover of darkness. They broke into his home so swiftly, DeStasio barely had his eyes open when the cuffs were thrown around his wrists.

Of course, since that moment, the man had been a kicking, screaming, livid mess. Charli and Matthew waited for him in the back entrance of the precinct. When they opened the back door to the cruiser, they found a grown man behaving like a three-year-old throwing a tantrum.

"Do you have an idea who you're dealing with?" DeStasio spat as Charli and Matthew each grabbed an elbow. The brawny man's emerald silk shirt was paired with silky black pants and black dotted socks.

Before this moment, Charli had thought silk pajamas were only seen in movies. She didn't think people actually bought and wore them. Wouldn't they slide right out of their bed?

"I think we're dealing with Marco DeStasio." Charli gently pulled his elbow forward through the doorway. "It's so nice to finally meet you officially, though I certainly enjoyed meeting you unofficially outside of Bernie Cobb's home."

This observation got DeStasio to close his mouth. The green flecks in his eyes, which were already brought out by his shirt, seemed to glow like embers with his rage. He may be infuriated, but he wasn't stupid enough to incriminate himself.

Charli had expected this. Of all the people she'd ever had to interview, DeStasio was probably going to be the most adept at police procedure.

And that was okay with Charli. Ultimately, they didn't need any further information to arrest DeStasio. At this point, he could say whatever he wanted. He was still going into a jail cell after this interview.

When they got DeStasio into an interrogation room, they left the cuffs on his hands. As the detectives pushed him down into the metal chair, he wriggled around like an earthworm on a hook.

"I won't be speaking to you without my lawyer present." Once seated, DeStasio finally accepted that he wouldn't be going anywhere anytime soon. His body eased.

Charli pulled her chair out, and Matthew followed her lead. She smiled at the surly man. "Oh, I expected as much. That's okay with us, actually. We were hoping you'd be more of a listener today."

Charli grabbed the tablet and gave it a short wave in the air.

"What the hell is that?" DeStasio licked his dry lips. Normally, they'd offer their suspect some water, but it wasn't like he could drink it with his hands cuffed. And Charli expected they wouldn't be in this interrogation very long.

Charli set the tablet down. "This belonged to a young woman named Candace Redding. Did you know her?"

DeStasio fixed the detectives with a steady glare, raising his chin in the air. If his hands weren't in cuffs, Charli was sure he'd cross his arms over his chest.

Matthew pulled the tablet toward him. "We figured that would be your answer. But maybe this recording will ring a bell." He clicked play.

Candace's voice floated through the device's speakers and filled the room, and DeStasio's mouth quirked ever so slightly. His chest rose and fell to the rhythm of Candace's muffled screams.

When the recording stopped, DeStasio shrugged. "Who's the screaming chick?"

Charli's eyebrows rose in feigned curiosity. "You don't know?"

"No, I don't. What a horrific thing to experience." DeStasio lowered his head and clucked his tongue.

Charli leaned forward in her chair. "I'll tell you what I think. I think this is a recording of Candace Redding's last moments. We know that you're very familiar with Ms. Redding. She introduced you to the Kirklands, right? You were interested in buying the funeral home?"

Silence.

The man was good—Charli had to give him that—but he wasn't good enough to escape a recorded murder.

"May I call my lawyer now?" DeStasio turned to Charli, a hollow smile on his face that stopped short of his eyes.

"Yes, of course, though I'm not sure what he's going to be able to do for you now." Charli rose from her chair.

Matthew followed her out of the interrogation room. Through the window, they studied Marco closely. He didn't move a muscle. A lot of perps tended to forget that they were being watched at all times once in the precinct, but Charli was willing to bet money that DeStasio wouldn't.

❋

In another interrogation room with Elwood again, Charli searched his face. If Marco DeStasio was night, this man was day. Like the day before, his hands trembled wildly. Elwood's teeth dug into his lip so hard, Charli thought they might bleed.

"What's going on?" Elwood's heavy breath punctuated his words.

"We've got DeStasio in custody." Charli didn't bother sitting down. She wasn't expecting this to be a long conversation.

Elwood swallowed hard. "Did you tell him I'm here?"

Matthew shook his head. "Of course not. We're actually good at our job, Mr. Sanders, which is why we needed to talk to you one more time."

Elwood's shoulders fell slightly. "About what?"

Charli wasn't sure how this request would go over, considering how terrified Elwood seemed to be. "We want you to testify against Marco DeStasio. We need a witness who will testify about burning the bodies at the funeral home, and we need someone to confirm that it is indeed Candace and DeStasio on that recording."

Elwood shook his head so hard he could have been a bobblehead. "No. I can't do that. Are you kidding? Those guys will kill me. I'm going to end up in prison right along with them. And then what happens? They'll have full access to me."

"Whoa, slow down there." Matthew put up a hand. "You might not end up in prison. Now, Detective Cross and I can't make you any promises, but if you bring all the information you have to the prosecution team, you may be able to be granted immunity from prosecution."

This was the most likely scenario. Elwood's statement was gold to the prosecution, and his information might lead to other arrests in this criminal organization.

Charli did her best to hide any disdain for Elwood. But it was hard to know that he could help get rid of so many bodies in exchange for cash and still live a normal life. She knew how things worked, though, and having Elwood on the streets instead of a mafia boss walking free was the better end of the deal any day of the week.

On a personal level, Charli knew Elwood was never going to be a threat to her once he walked away from this crime. DeStasio, on the other hand, was a cold-blooded killer who had already been following her and Matthew. If she was ever going to be able to sleep without one eye open, that man had to be locked away.

Elwood fiddled with his fingers. "If I can be granted immunity, maybe, but I'm not making any promises. This is my life we're talking about."

Charli figured that would be the detail to change his mind. "In the meantime, you'll be arrested for now but under protection."

"Under protection" primarily meant being put into an isolation cell, and that wasn't a pleasant process. But Charli didn't deem it necessary to explain further.

Elwood bit his lower lip once again. "Okay. But DeStasio can't get to me, right?"

"No, Mr. Sanders, you'll be safe. We can assure you of that." Charli excused Matthew and herself.

Once outside the interrogation room, Matthew let out a loud yawn. "I really wasn't expecting to wrap this thing up today."

Neither was Charli. "Do you have a feeling that maybe we got DeStasio too easily?"

When Charli heard her own words, they sounded silly. They'd heard the recording themselves. DeStasio's voice was clear as day, and Charli knew he was responsible for the murder of Candace.

But who was the other guy? And what role did he play in all of this?

Matthew patted Charli's shoulder. "You're just feeling off because we're rarely handed a win this easily. But relax, Charli. It's done now."

But it didn't feel done. There were still so many unanswered questions.

29

Charli turned to Matthew in the funeral home parking lot after shutting her car door. "You think Cobb is still going to give us attitude when we tell him his name is cleared?"

Matthew rolled his eyes, his lids hanging low from pure exhaustion. They'd been running on fumes for the last few days. "I think he's likely going to try and rub it in our faces that he had nothing to do with Candace's disappearance."

Her partner was probably right, but they had to speak to the funeral director regardless. They also needed to ask around and find out if anyone else knew about this body-burning business.

Though, if Elwood was telling the truth, only he, Jacob, and Candace had been involved. And it made sense that Cobb and the Kirklands were oblivious, considering Marco DeStasio was trying so hard to buy the business. If the owners and manager were in on the clandestine operation, there wasn't a ton of motivation for DeStasio to purchase the funeral home.

Animosity hung in the air as Charli and Matthew

entered the lobby. Cobb just so happened to be talking to the receptionist behind the front desk. As the bell on the front door chimed, Cobb's head snapped up. His eyebrows raised instantaneously. The receptionist's blonde curls bounced as she scurried into the back room. Charli figured she wasn't eager to witness the wrath emanating off of her boss.

The funeral director stood up straight behind the desk, slowly crossing his arms against his chest. "Well, I know you couldn't possibly be here to tell me Candace's hair was in the back of my seat since I know it wasn't. But I don't suppose you're here to apologize either, so…"

Charli hardly owed Cobb an apology. She and Matthew had done nothing but their job. Did the director expect them to ignore stray hairs in the back of his car?

Still, Charli would like this visit to go smoothly. They needed to interview employees of the funeral home, and Bernie Cobb had the ability to make that job much more difficult for them.

Charli plastered the sincerest smile she could muster on her face. "Actually, yes. We apologize for the inconvenience, Mr. Cobb. It's unfortunate that our investigation made your life more difficult."

The director's expression softened, and he dropped his hands by his sides. "So, you're not here to accuse me of killing my employees?"

Matthew's pale yellow shirt crinkled as he glanced over his shoulder to make sure nobody was about to enter the lobby. "No, we're not. Actually, we're here to inquire about something else entirely."

Cobb's shoulders stiffened as he pulled in his bottom lip. If he had dropped any of his previous suspicion, it had returned with a vengeance. "What is it now?"

Charli stepped toward the desk and lowered her voice.

"Has there ever been another instance where you found an unrecorded cremation had been done during the night?"

A crimson hue crept into Bernie's cheeks. "Of course not! What are you implying? If I saw ashes that were not accounted for, I would call the police as I did when Candace went missing."

This man was more than a little infuriating. Charli took a deep breath in an effort not to snap back at the man, and she wasn't usually quick to anger. But Cobb was, and the smoke was practically billowing out of his ears.

Admittedly, though, the fact that Cobb called the police in this instance was one of the reasons Charli didn't believe he was involved in the murder. If he was, he could have tried to get rid of the ashes and cover up these bodies as had been done with all the others, so what was different this time, and why had the ashes been left behind? Regardless of the answers to her questions, right now, she was simply covering her bases by questioning the director.

"Mr. Cobb, this wasn't an accusation." Charli somehow managed to keep her tone neutral. "But it's come to our attention that this is not the only instance where a body has been burned at the funeral home after hours."

Charli anticipated further rage from Cobb, but instead, his gaze began to dart around the room. He wasn't looking at anything necessarily. It appeared to be his way of processing the information.

When his gaze landed on Charli and Matthew, he shook his head gently. "That's not possible."

Matthew tossed back the dark tail of his jacket to slide a hand in his pocket. "Isn't it, though? As long as the ashes were gone by morning, you wouldn't know, would you?"

"B-but…" Cobb's words came out in a stutter. "But we have security cameras. We would have known if something like that was happening in the middle of the night."

"The security cameras weren't particularly helpful the night Candace went missing." Charli tapped her finger against her thigh. "Those responsible for cremating bodies after hours obviously knew where the cameras were and could avoid them...or turn them off and on when needed."

The anger had leaked out of the funeral director. He was apparently too shaken by what he was hearing to deflect any rage back at the detectives. "Are you saying that someone was regularly burning bodies here at the funeral home? And they knew where the cameras were? But that would imply... are you saying this was one of my employees?"

That was information they could not yet divulge. "I'm afraid we can't reveal those details yet, and since this is now a federal case, I'm sure the FBI will be knocking on your door real soon. You might as well spill everything to us first." Charli kept her face neutral, careful not to give any information away.

But he was already putting the pieces together. "Wait, not Jacob and Candace. It couldn't have been them. They were such good employees. But they..." He frowned, his eyes glazing over as he stared at the wall. "Now that I think about it, they always drove brand-new vehicles."

Matthew rubbed the back of his neck. "At this point, the details of our case are private. But we do need to speak to your employees once again to see if they know anything about who might have been involved with this."

And who the second victim in the cremator was, Charli silently added. That was still part of the puzzle too.

Cobb nodded emphatically, causing the jowls of his cheeks to shake. This was the first time during the entire investigation that he'd been so cooperative. "Of course. You can speak to whoever you want. But please, if you find anyone else involved in this, tell me right away. I just don't understand why Jacob and Candace would have done this.

What bodies were they destroying? Neither of them seemed capable of a crime so heinous. Were they murderers too?"

Cobb could continue to press for information, and Charli couldn't blame him for that. After the bomb they'd just dropped on him, it was normal that he would want to know more, but she wouldn't reveal anything else. "We greatly appreciate your compliance, Mr. Cobb, and you will certainly find out if any of your employees are involved in this case."

The director straightened his already perfect suit jacket. "Sure, okay. Thank you, Detectives."

When Charli and Matthew questioned the employees who were on shift, each one of them was horrified at their line of questioning. Elwood had insisted he wasn't aware of anyone else who was involved in the cremations, and that was appearing to be true.

Matthew held open the funeral home's front door for Charli. After the events of the week, she didn't protest her partner's absentminded act of chivalry. This likely wouldn't be the last time Charli walked through this door, but man, was she ready to take a break from this place.

"Well, we didn't think Elwood would lie anyway, right? The more people he brings to the prosecution team, the better deal he can get." Charli yawned as she made her way out to the parking lot.

Matthew answered Charli with a yawn of his own. It was at least his fourth one for the day. "Yeah, but at least we've got our bases covered. Now, I don't know about you, but I am damn ready for a nap. I don't think there's anything else we're going to do for this case today."

Matthew was right. There were loose ends they'd need to tie up back at the precinct, probably a few more people they'd interview to collect evidence, but that could be done later.

For now, it was enough to know they'd caught DeStasio. He wasn't going to be going anywhere for a long time. At least now they could rest easy without worrying about being followed by the mafia.

Though that had been just one of many worries Charli currently had. There was still the disturbing reminder that someone had sent a letter about Madeline to the precinct. Hell, someone had sent another letter right to Charli's door. Whoever was taunting her about Madeline's case, they knew where she worked and where she lived. The question was, were the two letters from the same person?

Charli let out a long sigh. She had to remind herself that, ultimately, her address was public information. It wasn't difficult to attain. And whoever had sent both letters had made no effort to make physical contact with her. If they hadn't already attempted to harm her, perhaps they weren't interested in doing so. This was a game of mental warfare.

"You okay, Charli?" Matthew cocked his head toward hers. He slowed his stride to match Charli's.

"I'm fine. It's just been a long week, and—" Her sentence was punctuated by a black Escalade with tinted windows pulling up directly in front of both the detectives, blocking their path to Charli's car.

Charli was immediately on alert, just as she could tell Matthew was at her side. They both took several steps back, both placing their hands on their weapons. Charli held her breath, ready to dive to the ground as the driver's side window began to inch down.

"Need some help?" Charli put a hand over her eyebrows to block the sun, so she could get a better view of the man inside. His jet-black hair fell right above his eyelids. Muscled arms bulged under his white t-shirt.

"Detective Cross?" The man lowered his aviator

sunglasses. Both hands were on the wheel, so at least she knew he wasn't holding a weapon...yet.

A shiver ran down Charli's spine. How did this man know her name? He wasn't an employee of the funeral home, that was for sure. Charli and Matthew had now spoken to every employee not once but twice.

Charli shifted from her right to left foot. "Again, can I help you?" Charli neither confirmed nor denied her identity, not that it mattered. This man clearly knew who she was.

"You could've, yeah. Not much you can do now, though." He popped the collar on his jacket, leaning further into the seat of his car.

Matthew stepped in front of Charli, as though on instinct. The move frustrated Charli to no end. She could fight her own battles, but she chose to ignore her partner. "Who are you?"

The man shrugged, causing his gelled hair to shift on his forehead. "I'm sure we'll get acquainted at some point, but that day is not today. I'm just a delivery boy right now."

Charli's jaw tightened, and her mind flashed back to the letters she had received. Was this the man who had been taunting her about Madeline? And if so, why would he expose himself like this? Surely he wasn't her murderer.

No, Charli had to shake off that hope right away. Nobody who had gotten away with murder for over a decade would be so careless.

"What the hell are you delivering?" Charli side-stepped Matthew, bumping his good arm in the process.

"A message. In fact, it's for both of you. Don't think about testifying in DeStasio's trial. I wouldn't recommend it."

So, this man was mafia. Wow, DeStasio was on top of his guys. Even after his arrest late last night, he still managed to rally the troops. And the troops didn't appear to be afraid of following through.

Charli could pretend she wasn't shaken to her core, but that would be a lie. This organization sure as hell seemed to have all their ducks in a row. Although putting Marco DeStasio behind bars had felt like a safety blanket at first, now that blanket had gone through a shredder as she stared DeStasio's associate in the face.

By putting DeStasio behind bars, had Charli actually put herself further in harm's way? The man likely had a whole team at his disposal. How many of them were at their boss's every beck and call, ready to harass anyone they wanted, including a police detective?

Knowing the danger wouldn't have changed the outcome, though. Charli had a job to do. Arresting Marco DeStasio was far more important than any danger Charli imagined she might be in. And she absolutely wasn't going to allow this thug to know that he had gotten under her skin.

Despite the gnawing in her stomach, Charli kept her head straight above her shoulders. She pinned the man with her unblinking stare, daring him to challenge her. "You can go ahead and let Mr. DeStasio know that we can't be intimidated."

"Really?" He slid his sunglasses back up his nose so his eyes were covered. But Charli still felt them boring into her soul. "Because I would hate to see you end up like your little friend. What was her name, Madeline?"

Charli's blood turned to ice in her veins. The blazing sun overhead could do nothing to warm the chill crawling down her spine. Though she was doing her best to maintain her composure, there were cracks coming through her armor.

"What was that?" Matthew scurried toward the driver's side door. "I don't think you'd be threatening a police officer, would you?"

The man let out a throaty chuckle. "A threat? I would never threaten a pig. You've got it all wrong. I said I would hate to see it. It's my hope that your friend there gets to live a long, healthy life."

The stranger didn't give them a chance to say anything else. With a squeal of tires, the SUV was gone. Evidently, he'd finished what he'd come here to do. Charli was pulling out her notebook, ready to take the license plate down, but there was none, though she made sure to note the "Escalade" imprinted on the back of the midnight black vehicle.

Matthew's brow pushed upward into a straight line. "Who the hell does he think he is? He can't threaten you like that and—"

"Matt!" Charli waved both hands in front of his face. She doubted anything but a physical action was going to grab his attention. "Maybe the way he spoke to me isn't what we need to be focusing on. Maybe there are more important matters at hand, like the fact that we're on the mafia's radar."

Matthew sucked in a deep breath. "Right, okay. But... Charli, if he knew about Madeline, do you think he's the one who sent you the letter?"

The thought had already crossed Charli's mind the second she heard it, but she didn't want to believe it. Not to mention the pang of guilt at Matthew's words that she hadn't shared about the second letter. She didn't want to admit that those letters weren't an actual lead but another dead end.

"I don't know. But I'll find out."

30

I slid my phone and belt into the box next to the metal detector, a process I was used to. This wasn't my first rodeo.

Though this one felt different. Normally, I was stopping by to visit organization lackeys who had taken the fall for bigger bosses. But to come see DeStasio in jail? It didn't sit right.

And it begged the question...if someone as powerful as DeStasio could be sitting in a jail cell, why wasn't I? When I'd heard DeStasio had gotten arrested, I waited for the cops to come knocking on my door, but they never showed up.

Now DeStasio wanted to speak with me, and I wasn't so sure that was a good thing.

After being cleared by a metal detector, I was escorted into a visitation room with three rows of plastic tables and chairs. But only one of those tables had a person seated at it.

DeStasio had one arm leaned over his chair. In front of him, a bottle of scotch and two glasses. Never before had I seen a visitation room entirely empty. And somehow, he'd gotten a name-brand bottle of scotch? The man had the world wrapped around his fingers, that was for sure.

DeStasio patted the table in front of him. "I'm so glad you could make it. Have a seat. I'm looking forward to a nice…chat."

With him, I never knew if I was being threatened. He could really be glad to be speaking with me, or this could all be a precursor to my impending death.

I took my place on the brown plastic chair. "Sorry you're in here." And I was, though it was better him than me.

DeStasio shrugged. "It's my fault." He took a long sip. "I should've listened to you about staying and getting rid of the ashes."

Although I wanted to say, "I told you so," I knew better. "No way of knowing the cops would have figured it out."

His mouth twisted. "Yeah. Doubt they'll ever figure out who went into the cremator first, though. Am I right?"

That was true. "Right. Nobody'll ever miss that punk anyway." I hated drug dealers, especially the ones who didn't know how to pay their bills. But that was neither here nor there. Time to get to the point of this little get together. "I was surprised you wanted to meet with me."

DeStasio furrowed his brow. "Why? Of course I'd want to speak with you. You're the best hitman I have. You didn't think I've stopped working just because I'm doing a short stint in the slammer, did ya?"

Actually, yes, I did.

"Of course not."

DeStasio grabbed one of the glasses and started pouring a shot. "I won't be in here long, so don't worry. I've got a stellar lawyer and no priors. And in the meantime, I want to make sure things continue to be operational. Here, have a drink."

I was more than a little hesitant to take a glass from DeStasio. He'd been polite to me so far, but that easily could've been an act on his part. For all I knew, the drink could be poison. But if DeStasio wanted me dead, it was a matter of time. At least I would get a ritzy drink out of it. I threw the shot back.

"It's smooth, isn't it?" DeStasio poured himself a glass. "I'm living good in here, let me tell you."

The elephant in the room was stomping all over my chest, and I couldn't take it any longer. "Why haven't you given my name up?"

DeStasio tossed back his head, laughter roaring from his lips. "Are you kidding? Look, they're going to try to take me down for Candace Redding no matter what. What the hell good would it do me to get my best hitman thrown in here with me? That benefits nobody. But if your name stays clear, you can continue the work for me. Like Elwood, for example..."

Shocker.

I'd known that was coming. Getting thrown in jail wasn't going to keep Elwood safe. He should've known that. I'd planned on hunting down Elwood without even having to be asked. I wasn't about to let him get away with snitching. He may not have known my name, but he knew what I looked like.

I flashed DeStasio a smile. "I've got connections with some guards who know where he's being held. I'll take care of it."

DeStasio smacked his glass on the table. "And this is why you're my man! We're going to continue to do some beautiful things together, my friend, just as long as you can get to Elwood before my trial. From what I hear, he's the prosecution's star witness."

"He'll be dead by the end of the weekend."

Marco DeStasio chuckled to himself as he swallowed the rest of his scotch. "It's what the little bastard deserves. Can't believe he went belly-up on me. And Candace, that bitch. I never thought the airhead would be so bold as to use a recorder. That was my bad. I was sloppy, and I know it. So, I'm accepting my mistake, and the time I'll be in the slammer for it. I'm just glad you did the right thing tossing that bitch in the cremator."

This was why I anticipated DeStasio rolling over on me. Technically, he hadn't laid a hand on Jacob, and if he gave my name up, he would have a chance at a shorter sentence.

But I was worth more to him outside of prison than inside of it, apparently. And they wouldn't be able to pin him for Jacob's death, anyway. He had a rock-solid alibi. We made sure whenever I did a planned assassination, he spent the evening at a public place where we knew they had security cameras. He'd spent that night at Lorenzo's Bistro.

DeStasio leaned back, stretching his arms out to his sides as he yawned. "Once we get rid of Elwood, my trial will be a piece of cake."

"And what about the detectives? Do you have any plans for them?"

One side of DeStasio's mouth turned up. "Oh, do I ever."

31

Mattress springs dug into Elwood's back. The lumpy mattress topping a metal frame couldn't have been more than three inches thick. Before his arrest, Elwood didn't even know three-inch mattresses existed. And this one was even smaller than a twin.

Elwood had never been one for luxury, but a sleeping bag on the bare dirt in twenty-degree weather would've been an improvement on this. If he'd known what dire circumstances jail would entail, perhaps he would've kept that confession to himself.

No, he had to remind himself that even the worst conditions were better than death. And if he was free, he would've been dead. If only he hadn't lost his damn passport, maybe he could've gotten out of the country in time to save his life. For now, federal custody would have to do.

How the hell did he end up here? When Candace first asked for his help and dangled the cash in his face, he'd taken it without hesitation because he'd never seen that much money in his life.

What was the point, though? He put all the money in a

savings account, anyway. At first, he'd bought a boatload of video games and a pile of weed. No more dime bags for him. Now he could pay by the ounce. But as it turned out, weed and games weren't all that expensive. And Elwood didn't desire for much.

So, there he was, saddled with a job from Satan himself, making money that never made him happy. And he'd had no way out of the gig. Once he was in, he was in for life. He could end his life, or the mafia could end it for him, and he had chosen to stay alive.

Elwood wasn't ready to accept his impending demise, though. He may not have desired much, but he sure as hell desired to live.

Footsteps echoed down the hall. With the concrete floor and walls, every movement reverberated through the vast building. When he'd first arrived, this barrage of noise had made Elwood jumpy. Eventually, he'd come to terms with the fact that jail was the safest place he could be. DeStasio and his guys couldn't reach him in here. Hell, none of the other prisoners were even aware of his real name.

In that regard, the detention center was nicer than the outside world. Elwood hadn't been able to breathe easy in weeks. Ever since Candace told him about her plan to ask for more money, Elwood's stomach had been in knots.

Her plan had been reckless. Didn't Candace know who she'd been working with? These guys were the worst of the worst, and they certainly weren't the kind of people who took kindly to ultimatums.

And what could Candace possibly still want? They got paid more money than Elwood could even dream of. Elwood had witnessed her greed grow, but he'd never understood it. Was the money making her happier? Was it actually improving her life?

Being flush wasn't improving Elwood's life. And he'd be

happy never to see a wad of cash again. If he could go back to the days when he was barely making rent, he would do it in a heartbeat if it meant no more mafia breathing down his neck and watching his every move.

Unfortunately, the men he'd worked for had made it clear that returning to his former way of life was no longer a possibility, and he'd accepted that. And as awful as this jail cell mattress was, as he tossed and turned and stared up at the concrete ceiling, a spring of hope formed in Elwood's chest. For many people, being in prison meant they had no hope for the future. For Elwood, prison was his only hope. As long as he was in here, he was safe to live another day.

One thing Elwood's money was able to buy him was an absolutely killer lawyer. And his lawyer was confident they'd be able to get a decent plea deal. Elwood was probably going to spend time in jail, and he deserved as much. He wasn't going to spend his entire life within these musky concrete walls, though, and that was what mattered.

After that, he'd get a new identity and a new nice life.

Elwood had his head all the way back on his mattress, eyes tracing the cracks in the ceiling. He'd followed one crack all the way from the right hand of his cell to the left, not stopping until his eyes finally closed and he sank into a dreamless sleep.

Ahem.

What the hell? Was someone in his cell?

It took a moment for Elwood's brain to piece the scene together because it felt so out of place. Elwood expected to look up and find an officer, but the shaggy-haired man before him wasn't in uniform. He couldn't have been another prisoner, though, because he was in plain clothes.

Why the hell would this stocky, six-foot guy be standing in Elwood's cell in plain clothes? A shiver shot down

Elwood's spine. He blinked slowly, as if that might change what he was seeing. It didn't.

Elwood licked his lips, willing the words to come out. "Can…I help you?"

The man didn't answer. There was a deadness in his dark eyes. His eyebrow dropped, but his mouth was in such a straight line, that his expression didn't change much. The lack of reaction only unsettled Elwood further.

He shifted up on the mattress so he was sitting up. His orange jumpsuit stood in stark contrast to the dull gray mattress and concrete walls. Even the man before him wore a gray button-down shirt paired with black slacks. Elwood's uniform was the only bit of color in the room.

Why did that make him feel like a target?

"Do you need something?" Elwood made a concerted effort to keep his voice steady this time. He pulled his shoulders back, as if sitting up straighter would make him appear more intimidating.

But Elwood was about as intimidating as a pile of dirty laundry. Besides lighting up a joint, he'd never engaged in any criminal activity before saddling up with the mafia. He was five-foot-six and as skinny as a telephone pole. This man could eat him for breakfast.

Hopefully, he didn't want to.

"I do. Need to chat with you." The man's voice was whisper-quiet, and Elwood could barely make out the words.

"Who are you?" Every muscle in Elwood's body was frozen solid. He couldn't move if he wanted to.

The man let out a long sigh as he reached down the front of his button-down shirt.

Inch by inch, the man pulled out a string of knotted together fabric. Were they…t-shirts? Elwood's brain was moving in slow motion.

He'd become very well acquainted with the scratchy,

bleached-white shirts the prisoners wore under their jumpsuits. But why would this man have so many of them? Did he work in the laundry room? No, that made no sense. Why would he be walking around with tied up t-shirts?

Elwood wasn't usually a slow man, but his brain was having trouble processing what was happening. Had he been drugged?

Still in slow motion, the stranger took a few steps toward him.

Elwood jumped to his feet, his hands pushed out in front of him. "What the hell are you doing?"

Slinging the makeshift rope over his shoulder, the stranger shrugged. "I thought we might want to talk more intimately."

Elwood didn't want to talk more intimately with this man. He wanted his damn cell door to open back up. Why hadn't he heard this man enter the cell? And how had he unlocked the door?

He stumbled backward. "Get out! Get out now!"

The man stepped closer. "I think we both know I'm not going to be leaving. I'm sure you get it. When the boss gives you a job, you have to complete it. My head will roll if I don't."

Gripping his chest, Elwood fell backward over the lumpy cot.

This. Was. Not. Happening.

Elwood had been promised protection. It was the only reason he was in this damn place! He'd traded his freedom for safety. Freedom was the most precious gift, and Elwood had given it away.

Was that all for nothing?

Absolutely not. Elwood wouldn't allow it. He wasn't going to die like this. DeStasio wasn't going to get him like he'd gotten Candace and Jacob.

Elwood didn't say another word. There was no time to waste. And since he wouldn't be able to pick a fight with this guy, there was only one way to make it out of this cell alive.

Pushing his foot against the back of his metal bed frame, he propelled himself forward. In a flash, he darted toward the man's right shoulder, with one hand held out so he could rip the cell door open as quickly as possible.

All he needed to do was make it out into the hallway. If he could do that, surely he'd see a CO who could come to his rescue. As he moved, Elwood took a deep breath. He screamed at the top of his lungs, letting out a primal, animalistic cry for survival.

As the man lunged for Elwood, he ducked underneath the stranger. The guy may have Popeye arms and a six-pack, but Elwood was fast.

When Elwood's fingers gripped one of the metal bars to drag his door open, his heart soared. The door flung back, and Elwood took a step out of the door.

Sweet freedom.

He could almost taste it.

In a flash, two strong arms wrapped around his throat. "Take another step, and I'll snap your neck with my hands."

Sputtering and gasping for air, Elwood felt the brawny arms release his neck and begin dragging him back into his cell.

"Ah, Elwood, I thought you were smart enough to know when you've been had." The stranger dragged him backward toward the mattress. "But you've definitely been had. Even if you could outrun me, where do you think you would go? How do you think I got in here?"

Elwood hadn't thought about it at all, actually. He hadn't had the time. His only focus had been on how he could save his own life.

"You think DeStasio doesn't have friends here? Even if

you made it to the next guard, he'd just drag you back out to me. It's over, Elwood. You should've known to keep your damn mouth shut."

Elwood's legs flailed in front of him, pushing against the metal bars of his cell. But the man's grip didn't budge.

For a brief moment, the vise grip loosened around his neck. He could breathe again. He reached up to rub his neck, but in place of the stranger's hands was a scratchy, knotted string of shirts encircling his larynx.

No, no, no. This couldn't be how he died.

"You know, I really didn't want to have to do this. It's a big hassle for me to kill someone in prison. We gotta make sure all the COs that are working are good with DeStasio. We gotta come up with an excuse for the security cameras to be shut down. It's all a big ordeal. I'm not a fan, but you forced my hand. You know how it is."

Elwood was yanked backward even farther, sending his head toward the ceiling. The trail of shirts had been wrapped around the light fixture above him.

This was it. The rope tightened around him as his feet began to rise from the ground. The room around him grew fuzzy as the last bits of air were expelled from his lungs. Then a funny thing happened. Elwood's brain grew foggy as a brief moment of peace settled over him, much like it did after smoking some good weed.

Maybe dying wasn't so bad after all.

32

Charli pulled up in front of Matthew's apartment Monday morning, wishing that the weekend had been a few days longer. She was tired, but that was mostly her fault.

She'd been obsessed with going through Madeline's old files again. After Charli told Ruth of the second letter she received, the sergeant had readily agreed to let her take a look into Madeline's case on her own time. It wasn't an official reopening of the case, but Charli would take anything she could get. No identifiable prints had been found on either letter.

Both Matthew and Ruth hadn't shied away from letting Charli know they believed the mafia was responsible for sending both of the nasty notes. The way DeStasio had been following Charli around, she couldn't afford to deny the possibility. DeStasio certainly had the connections to dig into Charli's past. Intimidating a detective was a very classic mafia move, and she hadn't received any letters since DeStasio had been put behind bars.

Charli couldn't let it go, though. Even if the most likely

scenario was that the letters were sent to mess with Charli, just the possibility that they'd been sent by the real killer was enough for Charli to look into the case once more.

And, frankly, in light of the ten-year anniversary, digging into Madeline's case once more was a relief to Charli. It made her feel connected to her friend in some small way. When Madeline's mother called, and Charli realized she hadn't even noticed the ten-year anniversary was approaching, she'd felt more disconnected from her high-school friend than ever before.

Charli wasn't going to let that happen again. Madeline was a part of her, one of the most important parts, in fact. She was the reason why Charli was a detective, and Madeline didn't deserve to be forgotten, not ever. Her memory was going to live on as long as Charli could help it. Whether she could progress in the investigation or not, she planned to move forward with it to keep Madeline close to her heart.

Picking up Madeline's folder from the passenger seat, she was tempted to open it again when she spotted Matthew coming her way. Charli placed it on the back seat instead.

She'd plastered a smile on her face by the time he'd opened the door. "Hey, stranger."

Matthew plopped down in the seat with a grunt. "Weekends are way too short."

She picked up the spare insulated mug she'd filled with coffee just for him. "Yes they are, but maybe this will help a little."

He grabbed the mug greedily, then cursed when the hot brew burned his lips. "You could have warned me."

Charli could do nothing but shake her head. "And here I thought you were a brilliant detective, Matt."

"The best." Matthew's grin slid from his face. "I'm afraid I've got some bad news about Elwood. Medical examiner called. He hanged himself."

Charli's mouth dropped open, and she thrust the car back into park. "But...he's the prosecution's star witness. What kind of case do they have against DeStasio now?" Anxiety rose in her chest. Marco DeStasio getting out of prison was the absolute last thing Charli wanted. Like she didn't have enough to worry about with the letters she'd been sent.

Matthew set his mug in the console. "Don't stress, Charli. They have a recording of the night in question. This is a slam dunk case. You don't need to worry about it. Anyway, I guess the guilt of everything finally got to Elwood."

Admittedly, Elwood did appear guilt-ridden about what he'd done, but Charli couldn't shake the idea that his suicide was actually a homicide. "Are we sure he hanged himself? That someone else didn't hang him?"

"The medical examiner swore up and down it was a suicide. I was thinking the same thing, but the kid was in protective custody. What are the chances the mafia could get to him?"

"Right. I guess you have a point." Charli's voice wavered. She remained unconvinced, but there was no point in arguing that now.

And, ultimately, the case was out of her hands now. It was up to the prosecution team to put DeStasio away. She could only testify as a detective on the case.

She had to put it out of her head. There was Madeline to focus on now.

Matthew took a tentative sip of his coffee. The way his eyes shifted, Charli could tell something else was bothering him.

"What is it?"

Matthew sucked in a breath. "It's nothing. It's just...I tried to do what you said and texted Chelsea a few casual messages. I got no response. I'm really starting to lose hope she's ever going to want to talk to me again, Charli."

Charli rarely comforted someone through physical touch, but she found herself reaching out for Matthew's hand. She couldn't handle the glisten in his eye. The only time Charli ever saw her partner truly upset was when he spoke of his broken family.

"I told you, Matt, you just have to keep trying. She's going to come around."

Matthew placed the mug back into the cup holder with more force than necessary. "But why? Why does she hate me? I'm really starting to think she isn't getting an accurate version of what happened between her mom and me. I mean, yeah, I know I wasn't home a lot. But the woman cheated on me! She's the one who broke our marriage vows."

Charli paused as she considered this. "Then maybe you need to find out what she knows. If she wasn't told the whole story, have you thought about setting her straight?"

Of course, telling Chelsea the truth could be messy. Charli knew the advice she was giving could lead to complications between Matthew and his ex-wife, but she couldn't stand seeing Matthew so down. He'd made mistakes, like any father, but he loved Chelsea. At the very least, he deserved a relationship with her.

Matthew's shoulders began to lift a bit. "Yeah, you know what? Maybe I will. I want a relationship with my daughter, and she deserves the truth."

A thought occurred to Charli.

"Remember the friend I told you about, Rebecca?"

Matthew nodded. "Yeah. You met up with her for drinks."

"Exactly. Well, I learned she is a counselor, and she actually gave me some really good advice about my feelings toward Madeline. Maybe I could connect you two and see if she might have some advice on how to deal with a teenage daughter. She could—"

Charli was interrupted when her phone rang. It was Ruth.

She put it on speakerphone so Matthew could hear. "Detective Cross."

"When will you be at the precinct?" Ruth didn't mince words, as usual.

"Uh, we're on our way. Why?"

"I've got another big case, and I need both of my best detectives on it. A local public figure has been killed, and it appears to be related to two other random murders. I'll give you more details once you're here. Grab Matthew."

"He's already with me. We'll be there pronto."

Matthew sighed after she hung up. "Here we go again."

For once, Charli was hit with a wave of disappointment at hearing there was a new case waiting for her. She had really hoped there would be some time for her to focus on Madeline's investigation.

Shoving the car into gear, Charli glanced back to where she'd tossed her best friend's folder before speeding away.

I'll be back to this, Madeline. I promise.

The End
To be continued...

Thank you for reading.
All of the *Charli Cross Series* books can be found on Amazon.

ACKNOWLEDGMENTS

How does one properly thank everyone involved in taking a dream and making it a reality? Here goes.

In addition to our families, whose unending support provided the foundation for us to find the time and energy to put these thoughts on paper, we want to thank the editors who polished our words and made them shine.

Many thanks to our publisher for risking taking on two newbies and giving us the confidence to become bona fide authors.

More than anyone, we want to thank you, our readers, for clicking on a couple of nobodies and sharing your most important asset, your time, with this book. We hope with all our hearts we made it worthwhile.

Much love,
Mary & Donna

ABOUT THE AUTHOR

Mary Stone

Mary Stone lives among the majestic Blue Ridge Mountains of East Tennessee with her two dogs, four cats, a couple of energetic boys, and a very patient husband.

As a young girl, she would go to bed every night, wondering what type of creature might be lurking underneath. It wasn't until she was older that she learned that the creatures she needed to most fear were human.

Today, she creates vivid stories with courageous, strong heroines and dastardly villains. She invites you to enter her world of serial killers, FBI agents but never damsels in distress. Her female characters can handle themselves, going toe-to-toe with any male character, protagonist or antagonist.

Discover more about Mary Stone on her website.
www.authormarystone.com

Donna Berdel

Raised as an Army brat, Donna has lived all over the world, but no place has given her as much peace as the home she lives in with her husband near Myrtle Beach. But while she now keeps her feet planted firmly in the sand, her mind goes back to those cities and the people she met and said goodbye to so many times.

With her two adopted cats fighting for lap space, she brings those she loved (and those she didn't) back as characters in her books. And yes, it's kind of fun to kill off anyone who was mean to her in the past. Mean clerk at the grocery store...beware!

Connect with Mary Online

- facebook.com/authormarystone
- goodreads.com/AuthorMaryStone
- bookbub.com/profile/3378576590
- pinterest.com/MaryStoneAuthor